Horace Helfin's Horrifying Halloween

Enjoy! 7-24-2012

Paulette Bensignor

HORACE HELFIN'S HORRIFYING HALLOWEEN

JOHN PHILIP McCARTHY

BOATHOUSE ENTERTAINMENT
LAS VEGAS, NEVADA

© 2012 John Philip McCarthy. Printed and bound in the United States of America. All rights reserved. No part of this book may be reproduced or transmitted in any form or by any means, electronic or mechanical, including photocopying, recording, or by an information storage and retrieval system—except by a reviewer who may quote brief passages in a review to be printed in a magazine, newspaper, or on the Web—without permission in writing from the publisher. For information, please contact Boathouse Entertainment, 1930 Village Center Cir. #3, Box #212, Las Vegas, NV 89134.

This book is a work of fiction. Names, characters, places and events are products of the author's imagination or are used fictitiously. Any resemblance to actual events, locations or persons, living or deceased, is purely coincidental. We assume no responsibility for errors, inaccuracies, omissions, or any inconsistency herein.

First printing 2012

ISBN 978-09614829-1-6
ISBN 978-09614829-2-3 (ebook)
LCCN 2011911878

ATTENTION CORPORATIONS, UNIVERSITIES, COLLEGES, AND PROFESSIONAL ORGANIZATIONS: Quantity discounts are available on bulk purchases of this book for educational, gift purposes, or as premiums for increasing magazine subscriptions or renewals. Special books or book excerpts can also be created to fit specific needs. For information, please contact Boathouse Entertainment, 1930 Village Center Cir. #3, Box #212, Las Vegas, NV 89134; 609-442-9523, or email boathse@gmail.com.

ACKNOWLEDGMENTS

I want to thank Beth Ann McCarthy, Jay Cohen, and Paulette Bensignor for reading the draft of the story and giving me their thoughts. I also thank Paulette for her artwork.

CONTENTS

Prologue 9
Chapter 1   The Goblin King 11
Chapter 2   They Went to a Garden Party 17
Chapter 3   The Transformation of Arthur Meney 30
Chapter 4   The Main Target 35
Chapter 5   The Candy Man 38
Chapter 6   Madness at the Mall 46
Chapter 7   Back to School 69
Chapter 8   Evil on the Wing 77
Chapter 9   School's in Session—The Battle Begins 80
Chapter 10 Somertown Is Warned 84
Chapter 11 The School Is Breached 91
Chapter 12 The Siege of the Gymnasium 105
Chapter 13 The Rock Lord 114
Chapter 14 The Journey to the Candy Factory Begins . . . 119
Chapter 15 A Friend and Foe in the Forest 125
Chapter 16 A Difficult Hill to Climb 133

Chapter 17	The River Crossing	143
Chapter 18	A Revelation	151
Chapter 19	Showdown at the Candy Factory	156
Chapter 20	Back to Normal	173
Chapter 21	The Goblin King's New Normal	179
Chapter 22	The Trick-or-Treat Ball	180
Chapter 23	A Comforting End	184

Glossary of Otherworldly Strangeness 187

Enjoy These Previews 193

About the Author 198

About the Artist 199

PROLOGUE

Sally Connors was closer to ten years old than she was to nine. Her life was moving along nicely. Thanks to her friend Horace, her parents were together and happy. Sally was doing well in school and keeping herself busy with sports and social activities. From time to time she wondered what Horace was doing. Her life had settled into a calm routine, but life for one of Santa's elves must be a constant whirl of interesting and exciting things. She was happy but felt she was missing out on some excitement. There was no reason for Sally to worry. Life is not always easy and smooth. Something always intrudes to cause a minor or major calamity. It was Sally's turn for a bump in the night.

CHAPTER 1

THE GOBLIN KING

"Horace Helfin must be destroyed!" the Goblin King shrieked in anger.

"Meeeowwww!" His black cat, Miss Mephisto, jumped in fear.

The Goblin King stood and looked down upon the flat, smooth polished crystal surface of the inside of a large rock that had been split in half and was lying on a pedestal made of petrified wood. The image projected on the surface disgusted him. He had just finished observing Horace Helfin saving Sally Connors' Christmas. Horace Helfin was Santa's top elf, and his successful exploits were monitored and resented by his enemies.

The Goblin King was disagreeable in physical appearance, temperament, and every other aspect. He was almost five feet tall, which was gigantic for a goblin. He was thin and bony but deceptively strong, with lean, sinewy muscles and large, powerful hands and feet. His skin was shiny and pale green and looked like it had been stretched tightly around his body. He had a square, muscular jaw and long, sharp teeth that were perfect for biting. His eyes were beady and black with no eyelashes or brows. His most notable facial feature was his bulbous nose. He had a cauliflower nose and twisted, deformed ears. A thin scar made by a sharp blade ran along his right cheek and the left side of his neck. A few large green moles did not distract the eye from his nose. His fingers had long, hard, sharpened nails that he kept meticulously manicured for scratching, clawing, and gouging.

His appearance was the result of a dramatic life. He was not born into royalty. He had taken it. His kingdom had been acquired through deceit, treachery, and vicious battles for power. He had been very successful in dispatching rivals but not without a few nicks and scrapes along the way. His current condition was caused by a favorite goblin-fighting tactic of inflicting sharp ripping bites to your opponent's nose and ears. Because of his size, strength, and vicious disposition, he had quickly risen to the top place of honor in his foul land.

His nightmare of a face was crowned by thick, shoulder-length blond hair that was beautifully combed and parted in the middle. He wore a golden-colored shirt of the finest spun excretion of the Bingbat Bug, which had the consistency of silk but was far stronger and protective. It could not be penetrated by a goblin triple-edged dagger or burned by a flaming arrow from an assassin's bow. The shirt was very long and almost reached his knees. His belt was encrusted with blue, green, yellow, and purple gemstones, which were mined from the Depraved Pit of Woe by his former enemies and rivals. The slaves worked sixteen hours before being beaten, yelled at, and humiliated for four. They were allowed four hours of sleep to recuperate for the next day's work. To his credit, the Goblin King did allow them two thirty-second bathroom breaks a day and all the Sulfur Plant gruel they could eat in a ninety-second dinner break. The right side of his belt held a long, thin knife. The attached scabbard was encrusted with the same type of gemstones that were on his belt. The knife's handle was made of gold-plated bone from the leg of the Cedabcast. This bone was the hardest known, and the handle was capped by the hard black shell of the rare Hibernating Hopping Heart Beetle. This grotesque creature was named for its preference, upon waking from a ten-year sleep, to hop on and quickly chew into its victim and lay eggs on the beating heart. The beetle and its hatchlings would then devour the heart and slowly feast on the remains of the unfortunate host. During his rise to power the Goblin King had used these beetles on a few occasions. It was always wise to have some Hibernating Hopping Heart Beetles in your arsenal and within easy reach.

The Goblin King snarled and turned to Miss Mephisto, who had jumped to the windowsill of the small dark room, which had only one burning candle. He walked to the window and began to pet Miss Mephisto from her head to her tail. The stroking calmed him, and he looked out the window at the land far below.

He stood at the top of a hundred-foot-tall decaying tree within his carved room. He scanned his depressing dominion. The landscape was dimly lit by a perpetual blood red sun that was intermittently visible through the thick haze. Strange creatures without eyes poked their small spiky heads from burrows in the ground and from knotholes in stripped and blackened trees. Volcanic ash covered everything and blew wildly in the air. Lava flowed from hills and hissed when it met thick bubbling sulfurous pools that released puffs of smoke when the bubbles burst. Barely visible bird-like figures flew awkwardly through the haze before plunging down to snatch a spiky-headed creature for a quick meal. Other bird-like animals made high-pitched squeals when they tried to steal the food from the successful predator. Lightning strikes continually streaked across the sky, illuminating the barren landscape. The crack of the lightning was followed quickly by rumbling thunder, sending the spiky-headed creatures back into their holes.

The Goblin King raised his right hand and made a fist. "The Goblin King will rule every world!" he bellowed.

He picked up Miss Mephisto, who purred contentedly. He carried her to the rock viewer, and they watched Horace and Sally, who were happy and laughing. The Goblin King was glum and pouting. He whispered wickedly into the cat's ear. "We will patiently make our plans, my dear Mephisto," he said, stroking her head. "Horace Helfin and his human friend will bow to me," he continued. "If they don't, they will be no more."

He reached out and touched a twisted, gnarled tree root attached to the back of the rock. He laughed with a sinister smile and whispered to Miss Mephisto again, "Our friends will keep us informed so we can strike at the most opportune moment."

The root ran down the inner trunk of the rotted tree. It ran all the way down to a dark cavern below the ground. It ran into a tangle of roots along one wall. An opened wooden door led to a stairway that went up to the surface. A lightning strike lit up the doorway and the wall. Two sets of eyes opened. Two sad, filthy creatures were barely visible. The bald, large-headed creatures were entangled in the roots and trapped against the cavern wall. The root from the rock viewer had split in two, and one end was embedded into the head of each creature.

The Goblin King became angry when the picture on the rock viewer became fuzzy and distorted. He picked up a hand-sized device connected to the thin root. "Seymour," he said. "Something is wrong with the Telesee-ers." There was no response, but he heard snoring.

The thin root ran down to the cavern and was connected to a speaker hanging on the wall. A small animal with the head of a ferret and the body of a small child was dressed in blue mechanic's overalls and sleeping in the corner of the cavern in a small bed. "Klauuu-skeeet. Klauuu-skeeet," the animal snored, starting with a low "Klauuu" and ending with a high, weasely "skeeet." "Seymour," the Goblin King screamed, and the loud noise blasted out of the speaker. The ferret-headed

creature woke up and jumped out of his bed. He shook his head and made a loud snort. "There is something wrong with the Telesee-ers!" the Goblin King screamed again.

Seymour picked up a sharp stick and snorted some more while he hurried to the wall. He poked the unfortunate creatures with the stick. "Yeck, yeck," he said as he poked.

The Goblin King smiled when the picture became clear.

CHAPTER 2

THEY WENT TO A GARDEN PARTY

Sally Connors put her black beret on her head to complete her young Goth witch costume and looked into her full-length bedroom mirror. She was dressed entirely in black, including her stylish new black suede hiking boots. Her black jeans and long-sleeve pullover shirt created the perfect look for any young hip witch. Green and black makeup was streaked on her face to make her look scary. Her blonde hair and blue eyes stood out among the blackness.

"Perfect," she said with a smile and held out her hands to look at her black polished fingernails.

Sally was excited because she had been appointed to a committee to organize and plan her school's Halloween Dance Party. She had been chosen by the prestigious Student Nominating and Organization Team, which was otherwise known by its acronym (S.N.O.T.). Sally wondered why they didn't just change the name to avoid this embarrassment. She didn't think about it too long because there were far greater mysteries to ponder. S.N.O.T had been politically correct and appointed a "Rainbow Coalition" of students from her class to represent all. Her school was hosting the dance, but there would be boys and girls from a number of different schools attending this big event. Sally was honored but knew that the planning would require a lot of work. She looked in the mirror and double-checked all the details of her costume.

Sally was satisfied and started to leave the room when her secret diary box mysteriously fell off her bureau and landed on the floor. Her diary had tumbled out and was open to the page describing the night she had gone to the Chinese restaurant with Horace and her parents. The blank fortune that Horace had received from his cookie was lying on the floor. She picked it up and immediately noticed that it now had writing on one side.

"Beware of false friends," she read. "That's odd," she said with a confused look.

She placed the fortune back on the page, along with the fortune she had received that same night. She placed the diary back in her secret box and walked to her bureau. The box had been sitting next to her Valakon, the toy elfin animal Horace had given her to bring luck when she would need it most. She placed the box down next to the toy. She stared at the Valakon for a moment. The cute elfin animal with the head of a Yorkshire Terrier, the body of a flying squirrel, and raccoon-like hands always made her smile. She raised her eyebrows because she firmly believed that the toy had moved from where she had placed it. She then picked it up by the collar and clipped it to the belt loop of her black jeans. She quickly walked out of her room and down the stairs.

She met her mother Amanda and her nanny Maggie O'Reilly in the kitchen. They were complete opposites. Amanda was tall, thin, and dressed in black, with free-flowing blonde hair, while Maggie was short, stout, and dressed in a white apron with black hair up in a bun. They looked like opposites but were perfectly complementary. They were preparing finger sandwiches for the first committee meeting being held in the garden sunroom. Sally chose this location to take advantage of the unusually warm and sunny October weather. When Sally walked in, Maggie was preparing the sandwiches while her mother put them on a serving tray.

"Great costume," Amanda said.

"Aye, 'tis a fine-looking scary arrangement of cloth and paint," Maggie said, finishing the last sandwich.

"Thank you," Sally said with a smile.

"Most of your guests are here," Amanda said. "I set them up in the sunroom with a cooler full of soda and plenty of potato chips." She finished stacking the sandwiches and handed the tray to Sally. "Here, you serve."

"Thanks, Mom. Thanks, Maggie," she said, taking the tray.

"You're welcome," they both said.

Sally walked carefully to the sunroom. She didn't want any sandwiches falling on the living room carpet. She was making safe progress until Stanley Kramer, dressed as a World War II pilot in a brown leather aviator skull cap with flaps, long white scarf, and brown leather waist-length jacket, ran into the living room and bumped into her.

"Whoaa," Sally yelled as two of the sandwiches hit the floor. "Watch where you're going."

Stanley's black hair was still slicked back but poked out from under his hat at places. He still wore his braces and was called "Beaver Teeth" because his teeth were growing at a rapid pace, and his nose still ran all the time. He was still the same old Stanley.

"I'm sorry, Sally," he said. He sniffled and took a white handkerchief out of his pants pocket and wiped his runny nose. "Where's the bathroom? I got here early and already drank two cans of soda."

"It's in the hallway," Sally snapped.

"Thanks," Stanley said and looked down at Sally's shoes.

Stanley was wearing his brown suede hiking boots, which were identical to Sally's old pair.

"Nice shoes," he said.

"Don't you dare copy me again and buy a pair of these boots," she said.

"What? No. I'm my own person. Original," he said and paused for a moment, looking at her shoes. "What brand are they?"

"Forget it, Stanley," she said.

"Okay, be that way," he said and moped to the bathroom.

Sally was a little angry about this mishap. She had been so careful, but Stanley always found a way to upset things. She placed the tray on the sofa table. When the sandwiches bounced on the floor, the top slices of bread fell off. She picked up the pieces, rebuilt the sandwiches, and put them on one corner of the tray. She would make sure these sandwiches would only be offered to Stanley. She walked into the sunroom to serve her guests.

The garden sunroom was filled with plants and had large windows that offered a beautiful view of the backyard. Beth Ann Yamamoto and Rodney Washington Carver were sitting on folding chairs at a round card table. Beth Ann was Sally's best friend. Her parents had been born in Japan, but she was from Somertown. She was very pretty with brown eyes, a round face with smooth brown skin, and a pert nose. Her long, black luxurious hair almost reached her waist. She was dressed as a young Goth vampire. As planned, she matched Sally's black clothes but did not wear a beret or makeup. She was holding her vampire teeth in her hand. Rodney was a tall, lanky African American boy with brown eyes and short black hair. He had prominent cheekbones and wore glasses with black plastic frames. He was dressed in a black suit, white shirt, and a thin black tie. They greeted Sally when she entered the room.

"Where's Sammy?" Sally asked.

"He's not here yet," Beth Ann said. "Typical Sammy. He would be late for his appointment at heaven's gate."

"Or hell," Rodney said.

"Here are some sandwiches," Sally said, placing the tray on the table. "Don't eat those in the corner," she said, pointing.

"Why not?" Rodney asked.

"I'm saving them for Stanley," Sally said.

"What—are they kosher?" Rodney asked.

"Exactly," Sally said.

The doorbell rang. "That must be Sammy," Sally said. "I'll get it."

Sally opened the front door. Sammy Sanchez stood there in his Day of the Dead costume. Black streaks and thin red bloody knife cuts were painted on his light brown skin. White chalk-like paint surrounded his brown eyes to make him look like one of the walking dead. His thin black hair was parted on the side and amazingly well groomed for someone who had recently died and dug himself out of the grave. He unzipped his coat, flashed it open, and smiled. He was wearing a black shirt with the life-size white imprint of the chest and ribcage of a skeleton on the front and the bony arms running down the long sleeves.

"Look at you. Good costume, Sammy," she said with a smile. She then frowned. "What took you so long?"

Sammy accepted the compliment but ignored her question. "Thank you. You're looking good too. You put a spell on me, you witchy woman."

"Shut up, Sammy, and stop changing the subject. What took you so long?"

"I had trouble finding your house, and then I was afraid of that big dog," he said, pointing to Baron Von Muncher, the neighbor's Rottweiler, chained out front.

"You always have an excuse, Sammy. That dog wouldn't hurt you unless you hurt him," Sally said. "Now, get to the meeting, Mopey McSlowpokey."

Sammy stepped in. Sally closed the front door, and Stanley walked into the living room from the hallway.

"Hey, Sammy," Stanley said.

"Hey," Sammy replied.

"We have sandwiches," Sally said to Stanley. "Did you wash your hands?"

"Sure," Stanley replied. "I always wash my hands."

"Okay, let's go," Sally said, turning toward the sunroom.

Sally and Sammy began to walk to the sunroom, but Stanley held back.

"You two go ahead," Stanley said. "I forgot something."

They walked to the sunroom. Stanley looked at his hands and walked back to the bathroom.

They were all eating, drinking, and laughing when Stanley walked in.

"Hey, save me some sandwiches," he said.

Stanley reached for the tray and avoided the sandwiches that Sally had set aside for him. Rodney slapped his hand away.

"The ones in the corner are kosher," Rodney said.

"I'm not kosher," Stanley replied. "I don't like that corner kind. I prefer that turkey and cheese on the top of the pile," he said, pointing. "I'm a very persnickety person."

"What does that mean?" Sammy asked.

"I've been working on my vocabulary," Stanley said. "It means I have very exacting standards."

He grabbed the sandwich, took a big bite, and turned to Rodney.

"I bet you a dollar I can figure out your costume."

"You're on," Rodney said.

"FBI?" Stanley said. A piece of turkey was sticking to his braces.

"No," Rodney said.

"CIA or lawyer?" Stanley said and sucked the turkey off his braces.

"No and no," Rodney said, shaking his head.

"MIB?"

"No. Not Men in Black."

"The black Roy Orbison or Johnny Cash?"

"What!"

"Who?" Rodney asked with a puzzled look, and everyone else laughed at Stanley's desperate guess.

"Never mind," Stanley said. "They're two of my father's favorite singers, and he said they always wore black."

Stanley put his hand on his chin and thought for a long moment. "Okay, Peanut Butter," Stanley said. "I can't figure it out. Who are you supposed to be?"

"You owe me a dollar, Beaver Teeth," Rodney said. "I'm Malcolm X."

"Oh," Stanley said. "Yeah, I can see it now. Why Malcolm? Why not Dr. Martin Luther King, Jr.?"

"I don't know," Rodney said. "I might change it up for the dance. I just felt a little angry and radical today."

"Why?" Sally asked.

"Aaaah, my sister ate the last toaster pastry for breakfast, and she knew that was mine," Rodney said, and everyone laughed.

"I hear you, brother Malcolm," Stanley said. "That's tough, but you have it good. My little sister keeps putting nail polish on my old action figures."

"That's nasty," Rodney said.

"Yeah, it's really messing with my head," Stanley said. "But don't worry. We'll both live. Pass me a soda, Malcolm Z."

"That's Malcolm X," Rodney said, looking at the cooler. "And I am not your servant." Everyone laughed except Stanley.

"Come on. I was just kidding. Give me a break. I'm going to choke on this turkey and cheese," Stanley said, grabbing his throat. "I'm going to need the Hein Lick Maneuver." Stanley pretended to choke, and everyone laughed.

"I'm sorry," Rodney said. "I was just trying to stay in character."

Rodney grabbed a soda from the cooler and held it out to Stanley.

"Orange, please," Stanley said with a big smile that showed all his braces.

Rodney shook his head, put the can back into the cooler, snatched a can of orange, and handed it to Stanley. "I'm only doing this so I don't have to hug you with that Heimlich. That's right, you heard what I said—it's Heimlich, fool."

"Thanks," Stanley said with a smile and took the nice cold can of orange soda.

Sally started the meeting when everyone finished lunch. "Let's start at the beginning," she said. "What kind of decorations should we put in the gym?"

"I say we go classic Halloween," Beth Ann said. "Skeletons, ghouls, ghosts, goblins, witches, black cats, clowns, vampires, jack-o'-lanterns—you know, the usual."

"Did you say clowns?" Sally asked.

"Yes," Beth Ann replied. "My entire family is afraid of clowns. Isn't everyone afraid of clowns?"

"Maybe we can leave the clowns out," Sally said.

"How about a Hawaiian theme?" Stanley said.

"Halloween is the theme," Beth Ann yelled at Stanley while everyone else chuckled. "What do you want to do—put hula skirts on the skeletons?"

"Actually, that sounds kind of cool," Sally said. "Not all of them, but maybe a couple."

"Maybe," Beth Ann said. "I guess that wasn't a bad idea, Stanley."

Stanley smiled a nodded. "Genius, I would say."

"Don't press it, Stanley," Beth Ann said angrily.

"How about flowers as a centerpiece for the tables?" Sally asked.

"Pa-leeeze, no flowers," Sammy said.

"Yeah, I don't like that idea," Rodney said.

"I like flowers," Beth Ann said. "They're pretty."

"So is a double-barreled chromed carburetor, but I'm not going to plunk it down in the middle of the table," Sammy said excitedly as Rodney nodded his head in agreement.

Sally and Beth Ann stared at Sammy.

"How about a human hand rising from the center of the table," Rodney said.

"Oh yeah," Sammy said and slapped hands with Rodney.

Sally and Beth Ann looked at Stanley.

"What?" Stanley said.

"You're the deciding vote," Sally said.

Everyone was looking at Stanley, and he froze. He reverted back to his safe old vocabulary. "I don't know," he said.

"How about we put this on the shelf for now," Sally said. "Maybe we could put lighted jack-o'-lanterns in the center of the tables."

"Now you're talking," Sammy said.

"Definitely," Rodney said.

"Let's move on," Sally said. "Does everyone agree that we should have a door prize, best costume contest, and a dance contest?"

"How many categories for the costume contest?" Stanley asked.

"Good question," Sally said. "How about best male and best female?"

"And best couple," Beth Ann said.

"I can live with that," Rodney said, and Sammy nodded in agreement.

"Band or DJ?" Sally asked.

"Both," Beth Ann said.

"My brother plays in the Flaming Headbangers," Stanley said.

"My cousin is in the Man-Eating Chihuahuas, and they are far better than the Flamers," Sammy said, pushing Stanley.

"No way," Stanley said, pushing him back.

"They're both garbage!" Rodney yelled.

"Enough," Sally said. "We can't agree on much, but I think we can agree that there should be no nepotism. It will tear us apart."

"Nepotism?" Stanley said.

"It means no favored jobs for family," Sally said.

"That's a good word and a good idea," Stanley said. "I will add that to my vocabulary list."

"Let's move on," Sally said. "What about food and drinks?"

"How about some booze, liquor, al-co-hol," Sammy said.

"Yeah," Rodney said.

"Don't you dare," Beth Ann yelled with wide eyes.

"She's right, Sammy," Sally said.

"Relax. I was just joking. You are such a pill BAY," Sammy said, using her nickname, which was her initials.

"What does that mean?" Beth Ann asked.

"It means sometimes you are hard to swallow," Sammy said, and all the boys laughed.

"That's it," Beth Ann said, jumping up and grabbing a potato chip. "Take it back, or I'm going to shove this chip up your nose."

"Calm down. Calm down. I'm sorry," Sammy said, holding his hands out in case Beth Ann charged. Beth Ann sat down.

"Pillbox," Sammy said, coughing into his hand, and Rodney and Stanley chuckled softly.

"What was that?" Beth Ann asked angrily.

"Nothing," Sammy said. "My mouth was dry."

Beth Ann squinted her eyes and pursed her lips. Sally stopped her before she exploded.

"Stop it," Sally said. "We are never going to finish this meeting. What about the food?"

"We should only have ice cream and cake," Stanley said.

"That's crazy," Beth Ann said. "What about veggies? What about protein? I need a good diet for my complexion."

"It's only one night. We'll eat like kings and queens," Stanley said.

"He does make a good point," Rodney said and Sammy nodded.

"I'm sorry BAY," Stanley said. "I'm putting my foot down on this one."

"Aaaagh!" Beth Ann screamed. She jumped up and pressed her open vampire teeth into the back of Stanley's hand.

"Owwww!" he screamed, jumped up, and rubbed his hand.

Beth Ann came at Stanley again and he ran for the back door. Everyone started to yell in great excitement. Beth Ann chased him. He made it through the door, but she slammed it on the white scarf that was wrapped around his neck and trailing behind.

"Ack. Ack," Stanley choked and held his throat.

"Open the door. You're going to kill me!" Stanley screamed.

Sally shook her head in amazement. This was the worst meeting ever held. Amanda heard all the commotion and ran into the sunroom.

"Beth Ann," Amanda yelled. She ran over, opened the door, and released Stanley. "What are you kids doing?" She helped Stanley back into the sunroom. He held his neck and pretended to be weak and faint. She helped him to the card table, where he sat down.

"Are you okay?" Amanda asked.

"Soda," Stanley said weakly and put his hand to his neck. "I think I need some soda."

"Oh, come on—give him a best acting award," Beth Ann said and started to clap.

Amanda went to the cooler and pulled out a can.

"Orange, please," Stanley said weakly.

Amanda put her selection back and got him a can of orange. Beth Ann glared at Stanley the whole time.

"Thank you," he said and took a long drink. "Ahhhh, that did the trick. Thank you, Mrs. Connors."

"Sally, what is going on out here?" Amanda asked.

"I'm sorry, Mom. We just can't agree about anything for this dance," she said.

"I see," Amanda said, looking at everyone. "I think it would be a good idea to adjourn this meeting. You should all think about what happened and have a second meeting with a spirit of compromise. Everyone cannot have what they want. You have to learn to work together, or you're never going to accomplish anything. The Halloween dance will be a bust, and you can all blame yourselves."

They all put their heads down.

"Can you all agree to try harder the next time?" she asked.

They all agreed.

"See," she said. "You ended the meeting with an agreement. That's a good beginning. Now, go home, relax, and try again later. But first let me get a photo."

They all stood up and moved to the front door. Everyone said their goodbyes and promised to work together as a team in the future.

THEY WENT TO A GARDEN PARTY

CHAPTER 3

THE TRANSFORMATION OF ARTHUR MENEY

Arthur Meney (pronounced "Me-nay") now worked for Sally's father at the Bertram Bell Advertising Agency. Last Christmas he tried to ruin Sally's family, but he was now trying to be a better person. He was giving to some charities and working on his greed issues. He was on a diet and working out at the gym but was still overweight. He had not met his goals but was still trying. Exercise could not reduce the size of his large head, nose, or ears. He still had his pencil-thin moustache and his cheap, brown wig.

Arthur threw the empty ravioli can into the trash basket. He could not even consider removing this delicacy from his diet. He sat down at his kitchen table to enjoy his lunch. He had left work to have lunch at home and was wearing his black suit, white shirt, and red tie. He threw his tie over his shoulder so no sauce would splash on it. He looked down at his bowl and smiled. He used his fork to spear a ravioli. He raised it up and opened his mouth.

Ding-ding. Ding-ding, the doorbell rang.

"Darn," he said, putting the ravioli back in his bowl. "That better not be the kid down the hall selling magazine subscriptions again," he moaned.

Arthur walked to the door in a bad mood. He had been waiting all morning for that ravioli. "What do you want?" he yelled as he opened the door. The safety chain was on, and he stared through the crack.

Shock was a mild word to describe how he felt as he stared at the Goblin King, who was wearing a long black trench coat and a black felt hat with a wide brim. Arthur looked down at Miss Mephisto, cradled in the Goblin King's arms. Arthur stared for a moment at his large green feet and wondered why he was not wearing shoes.

"It's not Halloween yet," Arthur said. "Get out of here."

Arthur started to close the door, but the Goblin King put his hand on the door and stopped him.

"Can I come in, please?" the Goblin King asked nicely but with a sinister smile.

"No," Arthur said loudly. "I told you to get lost."

The Goblin King pushed hard on the door, and the safety chain snapped. Arthur stepped back in fear. The Goblin King put Miss Mephisto down, and she nonchalantly walked into the room and made herself comfortable on one of Arthur's chairs in the living room. Arthur looked at Miss Mephisto and then at the Goblin King.

"Can I come in, Arthur?" he said with the same sinister smile.

"No," Arthur said loudly in a high nervous voice. "How do you know my name?"

The Goblin King stepped into Arthur's apartment. Arthur tried to back away, but the Goblin King reached up, grabbed Arthur's left ear, and twisted it.

"Owwww!" Arthur screamed as the Goblin King pulled Arthur's ear and led him into the living room.

"Thank you for inviting me into your fine home," the Goblin King said.

He let Arthur go. "Who are you?" Arthur asked, rubbing his painful ear.

"Never mind," he said. "Now be a good boy and close your door and come back and sit down. We have some business to attend to."

Arthur slowly walked to the front door and then quickly ran out.

"Meeeowwww," Miss Mephisto cried out and then hissed.

"Help! Help!" Arthur screamed as he ran down the corridor of his building to the elevator. Because of his fear and the resulting jolt of adrenaline shooting through his body, he was able to run surprisingly fast for a heavy man.

"Oh, my, this is most tiresome," the Goblin King said to Miss Mephisto.

The Goblin King ran after Arthur with great speed. Arthur was desperately pushing the elevator button when he was caught. The Goblin King grabbed Arthur by the ear again. "Owww! Owww! Owww!" Arthur whimpered as the Goblin King dragged him down the hallway. When they were back in the room, the Goblin King slammed the front door. He pushed Arthur to the sofa and sat him down.

"What do you want with me?" Arthur asked, rubbing his ear again.

"Fair question," the Goblin King said. "I need someone who knows Sally Connors and who is less than pure. You meet both of my needs."

"I'm a good person now," Arthur whined, still rubbing his painful ear.

"Aaahh yes, but you see, Arthur, I've been watching you, and I know about your—how shall I say—prior bad acts. I can tell you that I admired your past efforts, even though they failed. You did not know the truth about Horace Helfin. I can't fault you for making a good try," he said and patted Arthur on the head.

"Why do you care if I was bad?" Arthur asked.

"Another excellent question, Arthur," he said. "You see, I'm going to take over your body. It would be more difficult to do if you were completely pure. You know as well as I do that you have a good amount of residual badness that you never made amends for."

Arthur put his head down. He was not going to argue this point. "How are you going to take over my body?" he asked nervously.

"You are a genius, Arthur!" the Goblin King gushed as if Arthur was his brilliant protégé. He gently pinched Arthur's cheek and smiled. "Look at you, a genius among question askers." He stopped pinching Arthur's cheek and became more serious. "I can take over your body the hard way or the easy way."

"What's the easy way?" Arthur asked.

"Aahh, the easy way," the Goblin King said. "You simply close your eyes and invite me in. I will then easily jump into your body without violence or pain."

Arthur was scared, and his left eye started twitching. "What's the hard way?" he asked.

"The hard way is a little more difficult. The same result is achieved, but I have to fight my way in and take control," he said. He leaned in toward Arthur and smiled. "Which will it be, Arthur?"

"No! No! Please! Stay away!" Arthur said, holding up his hands and shaking his head.

"Very well, Arthur," the Goblin King said. "Hard it is."

The Goblin King fought Arthur's hands away and cupped his right hand over Arthur's forehead with a strong grip. Arthur struggled and then went into a trance. The Goblin King's body was absorbed right into Arthur's head. The trench coat and the black hat fell to the floor. Arthur's body contorted and went into spasms. After a few moments Arthur's body relaxed.

The Goblin King was in control, and he opened his eyes. "That was easy," he said. Then he made a painful face and grabbed his belly. "Owww," he said. "The idiot was so scared that he had a stomach ache before I took over."

He burped and stood up. "Aaah, it's gone now."

"Meeeowww," Miss Mephisto said.

"Right you are, my dear," he said. "We definitely should get started immediately."

He walked to the door and lifted his hand to his left ear. "Wow, that really is painful," he said, rubbing Arthur's—and now his own—throbbing ear.

CHAPTER 4

THE MAIN TARGET

Sally walked home from school wearing her blue jeans, long-sleeve white pullover shirt, light blue puffy goose down-filled vest, and sturdy hiking boots. Her backpack was exactly where it was designed to be. When she got close to her home, she saw a man standing near her front door. Sally's friend, Baron Von Muncher, the neighbor's Rottweiler, was barking wildly and pulling at his chain. When she walked closer, she was surprised to see it was Arthur Meney holding a black cat. She also noticed that Baron Von Muncher was sniffing the air, growling, baring his teeth, lunging, and trying to attack Arthur and the cat. So far the chain around his neck was holding him back. When Sally approached, Von Muncher started to cry and howl. The cat hissed at him.

Sally had a funny feeling and approached cautiously.

"What are you doing here?" she asked.

"Your father got sick at work. Nothing serious. He got dizzy and went to the hospital for some tests. Your mother is there with him, and she asked me to drive you to the hospital," he said.

Baron Von Muncher was crying and barking even louder.

"Is he okay?" she asked.

"As I said, just some tests. I'm sure he's fine," he said.

"What's with the cat?" she asked.

"This is my new pet," he replied.

Sally wanted to confirm this story with her nanny, Maggie O'Reilly. She tried to rush past him. "Let me check with Maggie," she said.

The Goblin King grabbed her arm. "I don't think so," he said. "Enough of this nonsense. You're coming with me."

"Let go of me, you freak!" Sally screamed.

Baron Von Muncher went wild. He was barking and making strong lunges. Sally kicked Arthur in the shin and punched him in the stomach.

"Meeowww." The cat jumped to the ground, and Arthur groaned and released her. He reached for her again. Sally removed her backpack and swung it at his head. The heavy bag, containing her large science and history books, connected solidly with the side of his head and knocked him back. She ran for the door, and he regained his composure. He quickly grabbed her from behind. He turned her around and held her by both arms as she struggled to break free. He was very strong, and she could hardly move. He stared into her eyes and smiled.

"Nothing can save you now. Horace will have to come to me," he said in a voice that was not Arthur's.

"What?" Sally said confused.

"Owwwwooh!" the Goblin King screamed in pain, snapped his head up, and his wig flew off.

Baron Von Muncher had broken his chains and sunk his large, sharp canines into Arthur's plump behind.

During the scream Sally thought she saw a horrible green face that was not Arthur's. It quickly disappeared.

Arthur tried to run away, but Von Muncher was firmly attached. Arthur spun around in a circle, and the cat hissed and clawed Von Muncher's hindquarters, but he would not release Arthur. His powerful jaws were clamped and locked. Baron

Von Muncher eventually twisted his head back and forth and ripped off the seat of Arthur's pants. Arthur and the cat ran down Sally's front walkway and down the street. Von Muncher chased him down the street, nipping at him the whole way.

Sally watched and was very confused. She ran into the house to check with Maggie about her father.

* * *

The Goblin King eventually escaped. Still in Arthur's body, he nursed his tender rear in a metal tub filled with ice in Arthur's living room. Miss Mephisto was curled up on a chair. A tuft of hair was missing from her back. The Goblin King was angry and silent, but he plotted the execution of the next phase of his strategy. He knew that in every war you could lose some battles and that this war was only beginning.

CHAPTER 5

The Candy Man

The Somertown Candy Company has been in existence for over two hundred years. It is owned and operated by Oliver Maximus Dribble VIII, his mother Cybil, and his sister Olive Minerva (a.k.a. Mini) Dribble. The Dribble family had made candy treats for the Revolutionary War soldiers. Their Chocolate Dribbles had been an immediate sensation. The rumor was that George Washington always kept some Dribbles in his saddlebag for a quick, sweet snack and that this energy sustained him on his famous boat ride across the Delaware. Oliver always went out of his way to emphatically state, with his arms flailing and voice rising, that Chocolate Dribbles had absolutely nothing to do with General Washington's famous tooth decay and that anyone who claimed otherwise was a perfidious liar, a scalawag, a scoundrel, and a ninny.

The Chocolate Dribble was, in essence, a convenient gold foil-wrapped ball of chocolate that could easily be carried and popped into your mouth. To Oliver and his family it was an insult to describe it as merely a ball of chocolate because the Dribble was an exceptional ball of chocolate. It would be like comparing a ball of manure to a ball of gold. They were both balls, of course, but extraordinarily different. "Which would you rather have?" Oliver would excitedly ask anyone who in complete ignorance referred to the Dribble as merely a ball of chocolate.

The Chocolate Dribble was made from the finest chocolate from all over the world. Oliver spent three months of every year traveling to foreign countries to meticulously find, sample, and acquire the highest quality chocolate and cacao beans. The classic Chocolate Dribble was manufactured by dribbling white chocolate over dark, followed by mint-flavored milk chocolate over milk chocolate with ground hazelnuts. This concoction was completed with a covering of plain milk chocolate. Other flavors were available, including plain, without nuts, for those with allergies, caramel, toffee, and nougat. The expensive Chocolate Dribble Maximus Supremo had a further layer of chocolate made from a well-guarded family secret recipe. Olive Minerva invented a smaller version of this product called the Mini Dribble.

Oliver was a gangly six feet, five inches tall, with a large head, long thin neck, and round face. He had a pale white complexion, and his white, thinning hair was always mussed. Matching his most cherished creation, his eyes were the color of milk chocolate and hazelnuts. He would tour the manufacturing plant wearing a plastic hairnet and would never comb his hair when he removed it. He was nearsighted and never took off his custom-made prescription clear plastic safety goggles. He also always wore his white smock with his name embroidered on the left breast pocket with milk chocolate-colored thread. In the smock's right waist pocket was a gold tasting spoon with the initials O.M.D. He inherited the spoon from the original Oliver Maximus Dribble, the entrepreneur who founded the company.

Oliver was forty years old but had a childlike way about him. He was always curious and exuberant and bounced around the plant with youthful energy.

Oliver was happy and proud that his factory was a major source of employment for the residents of Somertown. The large plant handled every aspect of the manufacturing and production of chocolate-covered candies. The Research and Development staff created new product ideas. Ingredients were stored in a commercial refrigerator and the warehouse. Large copper vats of melted chocolate were poured into metal storage containers, and the chocolate was pumped to overhead dribbling hoses that filled the molds, strategically placed on a conveyor belt. The vast assembly line of computer-controlled conveyor belts and related machinery moved along with automated precision. Chocolate was dribbled, nougat-covered, caramel-injected, colored sugar-sprayed, nuts-sprinkled, and fruit-dipped.

All products were visually inspected by sharp-eyed perfectionists. Candies with imperfect shapes, colors, or textures were immediately plucked from the line and thrown into a container to be taken by employees or donated to a food bank. No batch was released until a sample was tasted by the Supertasters. These employees had the most sought-after job in the plant. To qualify for this well-paid position, you did not have to be smart, attractive, nice, or know the owner. Successful applicants needed only one qualification: They had to have an extraordinarily large number of taste buds that enabled them to distinguish every subtle flavor of the chocolate. The Supertasters were hired by winning a tasting competition, and their tongues were insured for a million dollars each.

Once approved by the Supertasters, the batch was cooled to room temperature, packaged by machine, and shipped immediately. Only the Chocolate Dribble Maximus Supremos and the Mini Dribbles were packaged by hand.

Oliver could view his entire candy-making operation from the picture window in his office that was at one end of the factory and high above the floor. This gave him great joy. He was curious when he saw a bald man, carrying a black cat cradled in his left arm and gripping a black briefcase with his right hand, walking through the factory door. He was wearing a black suit and black shoes. The Goblin King in Arthur's body made his way through the plant and the maze of machines without asking anyone for directions. Oliver had never seen this man before, but he seemed to know exactly where he was going. He reached the end of the factory and climbed the high metal stairs that led to Oliver's office.

Oliver sat down behind his desk and waited for the strange visitor to knock. He was surprised when the Goblin King barged right in without an invitation and stood in front of his desk.

"Who are you?" Oliver asked. "Animals are not allowed on the factory floor for health reasons. How did you get past security?"

"Please indulge me for just a moment. I have a proposition for you," the Goblin King said.

"Be quick about it," Oliver said angrily. "This cat thing is a gross violation."

"My name is Goby King. I am a chocolatier extraordinaire from a far off land, and I want to buy your company," he said.

Oliver was shocked. "But it's not for sale."

"I will pay any price," he said.

"It's not for sale at any price," Oliver said.

"Very well," he said. "As a secondary proposition, I would like to sell you the recipe for an extraordinary chocolate candy. It is so exquisite, so delicious that you have never tasted its equal."

Oliver was intrigued. "I don't believe that any such candy exists beyond my factory walls."

The Goblin King smiled and placed his briefcase on Oliver's desk. He opened it and turned it toward Oliver. It was filled with chocolate candies. Oliver's nose twitched. He was excited by the smell alone.

"Uuuummm! What are they?" he asked.

"Aahh, an ancient family recipe," the Goblin King said. "One bite of a Delectable Dreamy Chocolate Covered Creamy and you will never eat another chocolate. You will convert your factory to make them and never make another kind."

Oliver was excited, leaned over, and took a big smell of the candy. "I must have one!" he said. "May I?"

The Goblin King smiled and held out his hand. "Of course, be my guest."

Oliver took one of the candies. He put it to his nose and smelled it, giggled uncontrollably, lifted it to his mouth, and took a bite.

"Uuuummm!" he said, sitting back in his chair and looking up.

The Goblin King smiled and nodded his head.

"Aaahhh, this is divine!" Oliver said. "I must have the recipe. We can be partners. The taste is simply sensa…"

Oliver stopped talking. His eyes closed, and his head dropped. He slumped back in his chair, and his arms fell to his sides. The candy fell out of his hand and rolled on the floor. The candy stopped, and the black liquid center oozed onto the floor. Oliver then raised his head and looked at the Goblin King. His eyes were bright red.

"Stand up," the Goblin King said.

Oliver obeyed immediately. The Goblin King pulled a pair of black sunglasses from the inside chest pocket of his suit coat. He walked over to Oliver and handed him the sunglasses. "Put these on," he said.

Oliver removed his glasses. He put the sunglasses on, and they hid his red eyes.

"Now we can get started," the Goblin said. "We have a lot of work to do. Sit down and relax; I will tell you exactly what you have to do."

Oliver obeyed and sat down.

* * *

Oliver picked up the handset for the factory intercom system. "Listen up, everyone. Listen up, please," he said.

"Shut down your operations. I have an important message."

He spoke in a monotone, his exuberance gone.

The workers on the factory floor looked up at the speakers hanging on the walls.

"Everyone, please stop what you are doing and meet me in the cafeteria for a special event. Thank you," Oliver said.

Oliver put the handset back in its cradle and looked up at the Goblin King. The Goblin King patted him on the head. "That's a good boy," he said.

The workers shut down their machines. The moving conveyor belts, swinging vats, and dribbling chocolate slowed to a halt. Packers stopped packing. Inspectors stopped inspecting. Tasters stopped tasting. Loaders stopped loading. Shippers stopped shipping. Everyone walked to the cafeteria, gossiping and speculating about the important message.

The Goblin King held Miss Mephisto, and Oliver stood behind a long cafeteria table. It was filled with Delectable Dreamy Chocolate Covered Creamies. Oliver held up his hand after all the employees had jammed into the cafeteria. Everyone stopped talking.

"Everyone, please take a sample of our new product," Oliver said.

They lined up in front of the table and everyone took a chocolate. After the employees took a bite, they raved about the taste, their eyes turned red, and they silently walked back to their positions in the factory. Before long the entire workforce was under the control of the Goblin King. Hundreds of tireless employees were programmed to start making the new chocolates that would destroy and enslave the residents of Somertown, including Sally Connors and Horace Helfin himself.

The Goblin King was happy. He carried Miss Mephisto to the center of the plant. He pulled a bag of black powder from his pants pocket, climbed the metal ladder welded to the side of a large chocolate vat, and sprinkled some powder into the vat. He repeated this process with the second vat. The production line started again, and thick black smoke rose from the vats. It billowed up to the roof in thick clouds. Exhaust fans were activated, and the smoke poured out into Somertown's atmosphere. The conveyor belts started to move, and the evil batch of chocolate started to be poured.

The Goblin King walked up the stairs to Oliver's office. Oliver, Cybil, and Olive Minerva were sitting on the sofa together. Oliver was wearing the sunglasses, but Cybil's and Mini's eyes were blazing red. Mini was tiny, thin, and pretty except for her new evil eyes. Her black hair was short and perfectly styled. Cybil was about eighty years old with white hair and a wrinkly face. She was five feet, two inches tall but thin and spry. The Goblin King walked in front of Cybil and stared down. He put his hand to his chin and studied her. "I think you will do for my next task," he said.

The Goblin King put his hand on Cybil's forehead, leaped out of Arthur, and was absorbed into Cybil's body. For a short second his black-and-white image was seen passing between the bodies. Her eyes were no longer red, but Arthur's were.

Miss Mephisto jumped out of Arthur's arms, walked to Cybil, rubbed against her legs, and purred softly. The Goblin King could not contain his glee. His plan was working perfectly. He stood up in the body of Cybil, cackled, and did a lively little jig around the room.

CHAPTER 6

MADNESS AT THE MALL

Sally was buckled up and riding in the back of her father's Jeep SUV. She was wearing her young Goth witch costume. Her parents were driving her to the Somertown Mall for the Halloween Costume Contest sponsored by the Merchant and Vendor's Association. Her mother matched Sally and was dressed in black. Her father wore his comfortable khaki pants and black polo shirt. Sally liked this outfit because it accentuated his handsome face, blue eyes, and well-trimmed black hair. She also loved black for Halloween.

"Did you talk to Mr. Meney and give him his hair back?" Sally asked her father.

"He hasn't been back to work since the incident. No one has an explanation for his conduct," John said.

"That's very odd," Amanda said. "I'm thinking about suing him for assault and battery."

"There was something really strange about him, Mom," Sally said. "It was like it wasn't really him."

"Well, as soon as he shows up, we'll clear up this mystery," John said.

They turned into the Somertown Mall, and the indoor parking lot was crowded. Every year it seemed that the entire small town came to the Halloween Costume Contest. After carefully searching, John found a vacant spot and parked.

Sally and her parents walked through the grand entrance doors and into the enclosed mall. The mall was decorated for Halloween with witches, skeletons, pumpkins, spiderwebs, and black cats popping out from storefront displays. The mall was crowded, and people flowed through the large space and were carried up and down the many levels on smooth, gliding escalators. Kids in costumes wandered around in anticipation of the big event. They made their way to the center of the mall, where the contest was to take place. This was a large open area with a soaring ceiling and big skylights that let the sun illuminate the space. Customers stood along the railing at different levels of the five-story mall, staring down at the activity. The contestants had to sign in with the organizers, obtain numbers, and pin them to their costumes. Next to the sign-in tables was a long Haunted House Tent that everyone could walk through for free.

Sally and her parents fought through the crowd and made it to the center of the mall.

"Go sign up for the contest, and then we'll do some shopping," Amanda said to Sally.

"Okay," she said. "I'll find you when I'm done."

Her parents went shopping, and Sally walked to the contest table. Stanley Kramer was standing in line. He was wearing his pilot costume.

"Hey, Stanley," Sally said.

"Hey, Sally," Stanley said. "Did you see Sammy or Rodney? They said they would be here."

"No," Sally said. "Sammy will probably be late, and Rodney is probably trying to decide what costume to wear."

"Yeah," Stanley said, looking around the mall.

They both signed up and received their numbers.

"Let's try the Haunted House," Sally said, pointing to the tent.

"I don't think so," Stanley said, shaking his head. "I don't like those things."

"Ahh, come on. Why not?" Sally asked and pushed his shoulder.

"You know I get scared very easily," Stanley said.

"How bad can it be? It's just a tent in a mall," Sally said. "It's not like it's a real haunted house."

Just then some younger kids ran out of the back end of the tent, screaming.

"That answers that question," Stanley said.

"Come on," Sally said excitedly and grabbed his hand. "They're just a bunch of little kids."

"Okay," Stanley said as she dragged him along. "But I don't like this."

The long tent was painted to look like an old haunted house with a decrepit front door, broken windows, splintered planks, and cobwebs. Large award-winning pumpkins with their weights posted were positioned to create a walkway to the entrance. The largest was gigantic and weighed six hundred and fifty-three pounds. On each side of the entranceway there were fake trees with evil human-like faces carved high on the trunks. As Sally and Stanley walked close, the trees' eyes opened, and their mouths formed angry scowls. Sounds of screams and moans came from speakers attached to the side of each tree. The moans stopped long enough for the trees to warn in loud, deep voices that the visitors should not enter but should run away immediately.

"Maybe we should listen to these trees," Stanley said nervously. "They seem to know what they are talking about."

"Don't be silly," Sally said, taking his hand and pulling him forward.

They walked to the tent's dark entrance, parted the fake spider web, and stepped in. It was dark inside except for one small light at the faraway back exit of the tent. As they walked, they heard the creaking of floorboards. They stopped walking when this noise stopped. Then they heard screams and noises that sounded like power tools. Moments of silence were interrupted by loud bursts of computer-generated techno music with blasts, taps, moans, groans, squeals, screeches, and staccato rhythms. There was fog and a smoky aroma in the air like something was burning. Strobe lights flashed on and off, disturbing their vision. All of the stimulation combined to confuse their senses, and they found themselves in a dreamlike and unbalanced state.

After Sally had pulled Stanley in, she let go of his hand. Stanley needed that reassuring touch again.

"Hold my hand," Stanley said nervously.

Sally took hold of his hand, and they slowly moved forward. When the lights flashed, they saw they were walking past alternating full-length mirrors and black curtains on both sides. They kept looking back and forth to each side because something was behind the black curtains. Unseen things were rippling the curtains and making them sway. Their imaginations were in overdrive. Stanley's sense of doom was causing his legs to tremble, and Sally was nearing that point also. The lights flashed again, and they saw a zombie with half of his face chewed off. They screamed until they realized they were looking at a mirror. They twirled around, and there was nothing in sight. Sally walked over and touched the mirror. They laughed nervously when they discovered that it was only a realistic painting on the mirror.

They continued onward and heard the creaking noise again.

"What is that?" Stanley whispered.

"I don't know," Sally said.

A light snapped on, and to their right side a grotesque hunchbacked man with a big belly stood staring at them. They screamed and then laughed again at this new picture until the man jumped out at them and screamed himself. He was shirtless and whitewashed from his head to his waist. An axe was sticking out of the left side of his neck. Blood was oozing out and running down his neck. He pulled the axe out, and blood spurted from the gaping wound and sprinkled his chest.

"Aaaahhh!" both Stanley and Sally screamed in high-pitched voices.

The man stumbled toward them, and they ran. They heard a woman scream. Another light went on, and a haggard old woman was sitting on a low stool, cackling. She was hunched over and held something on her lap that was out of their view. She kept pulling at it and cackling. She slowly turned toward them, and they saw that she was pulling the hair out of a disembodied head. She was carefully pulling one piece of hair out at a time. The eyes of the male head were open, and blood was around the neck where it had been cut. Sally and Stanley held each other tightly.

"Would you like to help me, my dears?" she asked sweetly.

"No," Sally said, and Stanley shook his head.

"Ahh-heh-heh-heh!" she screeched and threw the head at them. They screamed as the flying head came toward them. It hit the floor, rolled into Stanley's foot, and stared straight up at him.

"Aaaahhh!" Stanley screamed again, and Sally joined in.

They started running for the lights at the back of the tent. In the darkness they felt something on their faces like cobwebs.

"Eeeww!" Sally screamed. "Let's get out of here."

"You think?" Stanley screamed. "I told you this was a bad idea!"

They blew the cobwebs away from their mouths, waved their hands in front of their faces, and kept on moving.

As they got closer to the exit, an evil clown jumped in front of them. The white, black, blue, and red greasepaint on his face created a truly wicked looking clown. His face was painted white, but his nose was red. The skin surrounding his right eye was red and ran up to his forehead in a crude rectangular shape that veered to the side of his head at the top like a flickering flame. A similar but smaller triangle was under his eye, running down his cheek. This pattern was repeated on the left side of his face but in blue. Black veins meandered down the center of his forehead, the sides of his head, and from ear to ear running down and under his mouth. His lips were deathly black. He smiled, exposing his sharp yellowy white teeth that were highlighted by his bright red gums. A tuft of white hair on top of his head stood straight up.

Sally was really worried. There was something about this character that was different than the others. She sensed real danger. Maybe she was wrong, but her intuition told her that there was something really strange about his bright red eyes. There was no way she would share her concern with Stanley. He was wobbly with fear and falling apart already. She thought that she must be wrong. This was only a make-believe Halloween Haunted House. She calmed herself and joined Stanley in action. They each ducked under one of his grabbing arms. Stanley stumbled over his giant floppy shoe and fell. Sally ran back to help him as the slow-moving clown turned.

"Are you all right?" Sally asked.

"I'm fine. Let's go," Stanley said.

The clown reached to grab them, but he was not quick enough. Stanley avoided him at the last moment, and they started running again. They ran to the light, but then it turned off.

HORACE HELFIN'S HORRIFYING HALLOWEEN

"What happened?" Stanley asked.

"I don't know," Sally said. "Be careful and walk slowly."

After a few steps they began to walk up an incline.

"Do you feel that?" Stanley asked.

"Yeah. Keep moving," Sally said.

The incline stopped, and they were on level ground. A light went on. They were standing on a black wooden platform. They had walked up a ramp and had to go down a ramp to get out of the tent. Sally looked around.

"Be careful," she said, pointing down at the floor. "There are some holes in this platform."

Music started to blare with intermittent sounds of chainsaws, dentist drills, screaming, sledgehammers, and rattling chains. Stanley let out a low scream and started chanting, "It's not real." The lights flashed on and off, and the platform started to shake. Stanley immediately stopped his chant. Sally and Stanley put their hands on each other to keep their balance.

They both screamed when a big man stepped out of the shadows and started walking up the ramp in front of them.

He was bald and fat. A light brown leather mask was tied on his face, and he wore the same color leather apron. His red eyes were visible through the cut-out holes of the mask.

"Uuhgg. Uuhgg," he grunted.

His top and bottom lips were pierced with the bolt of a lock. The lock was closed, and he could not open his mouth. His bare arms were covered with thick black hair. He lifted his right hand, and he held a bloody axe.

"I can't move," Stanley whimpered.

"Get over it, Stanley. We have to get out of here!" Sally screamed.

"No. I mean something's got me," Stanley said.

Sally looked down. A pair of lizard-like hands had emerged from the holes in the platform and grabbed Stanley's legs. As the man walked closer, Sally grabbed Stanley and pulled. The hands did not release Stanley, and the axe murderer slowly moved closer. Sally threw her weight into it and pulled harder. The hands released him, and they both fell on the platform. They looked up: The fat man was five feet away from them. They screamed as the fat man growled. They stood up and, with a fear-fueled burst of speed, ran around the man to the back exit of the tent. A swirling vortex of light was projected over the back flap of the tent. They ran full force into the back of the tent and sent the flap flying open. They came bursting into the sunny mall and screamed until they were a safe distance away.

They were still scared and breathing hard. Stanley hugged Sally. He then backed away, putting his hand on his chest.

"That was pretty bad. My heart is still racing," he said. "Call 911 if I collapse."

"It was scarier than I thought it would be," Sally said.

She looked at Stanley and started to nervously laugh. After a moment, he started to laugh too. Some screams drew their attention to the exit of the tent. They both laughed, but Sally stopped. She still had a funny feeling about that Haunted Tent and the red-eyed men.

"Let's watch some other kids come out," Stanley said.

Sally smiled and nodded her head. They heard some more screams, and soon some wild-eyed kids bolted out of the tent.

They watched another group of terrified kids run out of the tent, and then they saw Rodney and Sammy signing up for the contest. Rodney was now wearing the same costume as Sammy. He was not wearing glasses. Their identical skeleton bone shirts were sewn together. They stood side by side and were attached for about six inches between the waist and chest. They were dressed as Day of the Dead Siamese twins. It was a great costume, but Rodney was about four inches taller than Sammy, and they seemed off balance.

"Great costume," Stanley said.

"Thanks," Rodney said. "I decided to change it up. We came up with this idea. Pretty good, huh?"

"Sammy, if you wore platform shoes, the costume would be perfect," Sally said.

"We thought of that," Sammy said. "But it's pretty obvious that we're not identical Siamese twins. Our differences make it funnier."

"You're right; it does," Sally said after thinking about it for a moment.

"When does the contest start?" Stanley asked.

"In about an hour," Rodney replied.

"Anybody see Beth Ann?" Sally asked. "She was supposed to meet me here."

Rodney looked at Sammy, and they shook their heads. "No. We haven't seen her," Rodney said.

"Let's walk around and check things out," Sally said. "I'm sure she'll be here before the contest starts."

The contest organizers were giving out free candy corn. They all grabbed big handfuls from large bowls and stuffed their pockets for the stroll around the mall. They ran up the steps to the second level and walked around, observing the scene. Kids were dressed in every imaginable costume. There was every shape and size of witch, ghost, goblin, ghoul, superhero, celebrity, doctor, nurse, politician, serial killer, psychopath, animal, vegetable, product, and thing. Sally particularly liked the young boy dressed as a lunchbox, holding hands with his little brother, the thermos, and his tiny sister, the lunchmeat sandwich with lettuce and tomato. She felt they could go far in the competition because of the cuteness factor alone.

They walked around the mall and checked out the stores for the latest computer games, shoes, and clothing. They passed the food court, and Sally saw Beth Ann sitting at the back in a far corner. She was wearing her vampire costume.

"Wait a minute, guys," Sally said and ran into the food court.

Beth Ann's vampire teeth lay on the table as she gobbled down the last few bites of a big corndog.

"No salad?" Sally asked as she reached the table.

"I love these things," Beth Ann said with a guilty look. "I have to get my fix every once in a while. I am so bad."

"Come on," Sally said. "We're walking the mall before the contest starts."

Beth Ann finished eating, wiped her mouth with her napkin, and stood up. "Let's go," she said while throwing her trash in the nearest can. "And Sally."

"What?" Sally asked.

"This unhealthy food can be our secret," Beth Ann said, holding her finger to her lips and looking out of the food court.

Sally turned around; the guys were waving and motioning for them to come out.

"Gotcha," Sally said, tapping her nose with her index finger, which was their signal for keeping a secret.

They both laughed and walked out to join the boys.

* * *

The Goblin King, in the body of Cybil Dribble, had set up his kiosk and tables next to the Halloween Haunted House Tent. A sign overtop his stand read: "FREE SAMPLES—DELECTABLE DREAMY CHOCOLATE COVERED CREAMIES—THE NEW TASTE SENSATION FROM THE MAKERS OF THE CHOCOLATE DRIBBLE." Bowls of the candy were lined along the tables, and employees wearing sunglasses held out silver trays with candy on white paper doilies.

"Adults only!" the Goblin King cried out in Cybil's high voice. "Children may have some after the costume contest." He held Miss Mephisto in his arms, and she purred as he stroked her. "Destroy the leaders and the children will follow," he whispered in her ear.

As Sally and her friends walked along the second-level promenade, she noticed something odd. Seymour walked toward her, drinking from a large soda cup with a straw and eating a soft pretzel. She stared as he walked past and bumped into her. "Yech. Yech," he said, looking up at her.

"Excuse me," Sally said sarcastically and stared at him as he walked away. "Did you see that strange kid?" she asked Beth Ann.

"I didn't see anything," Beth Ann replied.

"There was something weird about that kid," Sally said. She turned around to see where he went, but he was gone. "But he will definitely win the contest," she said, turning back to Beth Ann.

"Hey, check this out!" Rodney yelled. Rodney, Sammy, and Stanley were looking over the railing.

Sally and Beth Ann ran over and joined the boys. A large crowd had gathered around the Goblin King's tables.

"Hey, there are my parents," Sally said. "Mom. Dad," she yelled, waving, but they did not hear her.

"What's going on?" Stanley asked.

"I don't know," Sammy said. "But we should go find out."

"Let's go," Sally said—and they all started running.

They ran down the escalator, dodged through the other people, and made their way to the center of the mall. When they got closer to the Goblin King, they slowed to a walk, and Sally sensed that something was wrong. Adults were wandering around aimlessly, and they had red eyes.

"What's with these people?" Sally asked her friends.

"I don't know," Stanley said, sniffling.

"Maybe they have the flu," Beth Ann said.

"But look at their eyes," Sammy said.

"Yeah, that's super-spooky," Rodney said.

"Something's definitely wrong," Sally said.

Sally saw the Goblin King's sign from a distance. She noticed that people were taking samples of the candy, staggering for a moment, and then walking away with red eyes.

"It's the candy," Sally said.

"What?" Beth Ann asked.

"There's something wrong with that candy," Sally replied.

Sally looked around and saw her parents. She became very frightened because a man in sunglasses held a tray out to them, and they were both taking a piece of candy.

"Don't eat that candy!" she screamed as loud as she could and started running to her parents. Her friends followed. Adults with red eyes grabbed at them and slowed them down as they pulled away and ducked under the groping hands. Sally finally made it to her parents, but their backs were turned toward her. She shouted out a warning.

"Mom! Dad! Don't eat that candy!"

She was upon them. She reached up and touched their backs. They turned around slowly, and their eyes were red.

"No!" Sally screamed.

Her parents grabbed her. She struggled to get away. Her friends were confused, and Stanley was scared.

"What's going on, Sally?" he yelled.

"I don't know," Sally said as she struggled. "But something bad is happening."

Her friends watched her struggle to get free from her parents' grasp. They didn't know what to do.

The Goblin King walked up to Sally with a bowl of candy. Seymour walked next to him, holding Miss Mephisto.

"Just the person I was looking for," the Goblin King said in his sweet-old-lady voice and with a charming look.

"Who are you?" Sally asked as she stopped struggling with her parents for a moment.

"I'm the person who is going to make you eat this nice piece of chocolate," he laughed, holding up the piece of candy.

Sally knew this was no kindly old lady.

"Yeck. Yeck," Seymour said, and Miss Mephisto meowed.

"Leave her alone," Stanley yelled, and the others backed him up.

As the Goblin King waved his hand in the air, his employees with the sunglasses stopped what they were doing and turned toward Sally's friends. The employees walked forward, and Sally's friends stepped backward. They looked at each other. They were surprised and confused and still didn't know what to do.

"Uh oh," Stanley said.

"Now, eat up," the Goblin King said, jamming the chocolate into Sally's face.

Sally clamped her mouth shut and would not open it. The Goblin King jammed it at her mouth. Her black beret fell off when she turned her head from side to side. He kept trying, and the chocolate streaked over her face and smeared her makeup, but she would not open her mouth. The Goblin King became very angry.

"Open it!" the Goblin King said to Sally's parents.

John held Sally as Amanda tried to pry Sally's mouth open with her fingers. Sally continued to struggle to free herself.

"No, Mom!" she cried. "You don't know what you're doing!"

She clamped her mouth shut as the Goblin King jammed the candy into her face again. The employees moved closer, and Sally's friends ran around and dodged them.

Sally was about to give up. She was surprised at the strength and stamina of this old woman. Her muscles were tiring. She looked up to the ceiling of the mall—something was happening. She thought she was hallucinating. Large bubbles were forming on the surface of the high ceiling like paint blistering under a blowtorch. The bubbles then started to form in the air below the ceiling. Froth formed at the edge of the circle of bubbles that kept expanding. It looked like soda bubbling and frothing after being poured into a glass. This was happening from the ceiling coming downward. It started out with the white color of the ceiling but was now turning light blue with a light green tint around the foaming edges. The sunlight from the skylights passed through the bubbling translucent mass. A slight hissing noise was heard when the bubbling, frothing circle grew to about twenty feet in diameter. Sally's friends heard the noise, and they looked up. They were shocked when they saw it.

Horace Helfin plunged through the bubbling foam, landing feet first in the new dimension. He was wearing his red shirt, which matched his red-haired head, blue jeans, and black boots. He was quickly followed by a blond-haired elf dressed in a green shirt, blue jeans, and black boots who landed beside him. They were in human form and did not have pointed ears. Horace grabbed his blond-haired partner and threw him feet first at the Goblin King. The flying elf landed on the Goblin King, scissoring his neck with his legs and kicking Sally's parents away at the same time. He squeezed his thighs against the Goblin King's neck, grabbed his old white hair, and held on tight. The Goblin King couldn't breathe and spun around and around, trying to throw off the elf. He tried to pull the legs off his neck. He could not remove the elf, and his frantic twirling slowed and then stopped. The Goblin King passed out from lack of oxygen and fell to the ground. While this was happening, Horace ran to tackle Seymour, and Miss Mephisto hissed and jumped. Seymour crashed to the floor with Horace on top of him. Horace jumped up. He lifted the dazed Seymour up by his legs and stuffed him headfirst into a trashcan. A muffled "Yeck, yeck" was heard.

Slow to react but now moving fast, the men with the sunglasses attacked Sally, her friends, Horace, and his partner. Sally and her friends pelted them in the face with candy corn and ran. Horace and his partner battled the attackers and held them off.

Recognizing the enormity of the threat and thinking quickly, Sally warned the other kids and offered a gathering place of safety.

"Stay away from the red-eyed adults, even if they're your parents!" she yelled to every kid as she used her hand to wipe the chocolate off her face as she ran. "Make your way back to the school. Pass it on."

Sally's friends joined in the warning, and the message spread quickly. Horace and his partner ran to join Sally and her friends.

Sally turned and took one last sad look at her parents and then ran with her friends to the entrance to the Somers Department Store. The bald, fat man with the leather mask and locked mouth from the Haunted House jumped from a hiding place and swung his axe at Sally's head. She ducked at the last moment, and the axe swooshed over her head. Horace punched the man in the stomach, and he doubled over in pain, sucking for air.

From the mall they ran through the opening and into the department store. The men with sunglasses and the evil clown were close behind. Upon entering the store, Horace quickly looked around. He ran over to a bucket on wheels with a mop in it.

"Hide!" he yelled to the others.

Horace took the mop out and poured the bucket of soapy water on the white marble floor at the entrance to the store.

The pursuers in sunglasses began to slide on the wet floor. One by one they fell to the floor and piled up on each other. The evil clown snuck around the wet spot and tried to grab Horace from behind. Horace's partner rolled the bucket at the clown. Like a bowling ball striking a pin, it knocked the clown over, leaving him rolling in the soapy water.

Horace and his friend ran into the store.

The axe man had recovered and cornered Rodney and Sammy in front of the escalator. He was grunting, growling, and snorting as he approached with his axe held high in his right hand.

"Run!" Rodney screamed.

He swung the axe, and they tried to run in opposite directions. Their costume stretched out as the axe man split them in half. Rodney and Sammy fell down. The axe man's momentum carried him onto the escalator, and he tumbled down the steps.

Sally and Beth Ann were hiding in the cosmetic department. Sally used a towel she had grabbed from the bed-and-bath department to clean the remaining chocolate and makeup off her face and hands. A man wearing sunglasses and a black suit teamed up with the wet evil clown and searched for them. Beth Ann ducked behind a sales counter, and Sally ran a few aisles away. She stood next to a mannequin dressed as a witch. She grabbed the mannequin's broomstick, placed the black witch's hat on her head, and stood perfectly still.

Beth Ann peeked up over the counter and saw the clown moving in her direction. Her eyes grew wide, and she sat down behind the counter. She pressed her hands together in a praying motion and rocked back and forth.

"Oh no. Oh no. No. No. No," she whispered quietly. "I hate clowns."

She composed herself and started looking through the shelves under the counter. She opened a big metal container of white powder and some got into her nose.

"Aachhoo!" she sneezed, trying to stifle it and keep the noise down.

The evil clown turned toward the noise. He walked to the sales counter and slowly looked over. Beth Ann threw a handful of powder into his face. The clown stepped back, the powder covering his face, and shook his head. Beth Ann threw the remaining powder at him. It came out of the container like water from a bucket and smashed into his face again. This large volume of powder covered his face and piled up on his head and shoulders like the worst case of dandruff that ever existed. He sneezed, coughed, and tried to rub the powder from his eyes. Powder spurted out with each cough. Beth Ann climbed over the counter. While the clown was blinded, she clubbed him on the head with the empty container. The impact made a loud gong sound, and the clown went down. Beth Ann looked at the clown with disgust.

"I hate clowns," she said and ran away.

The man with sunglasses walked close to Sally, who stood motionless. He stood in front of the mannequin and stared into the face. He slowly reached up and touched the cheek. Sally didn't budge. He turned to Sally, bent down closer to her face, and stared. He slowly reached up to touch her cheek, and she quickly bopped him on the head with the witch's broomstick. The startled man stood up and rubbed his painful head. Sally immediately poked him in the belly with the end of the broom. He grabbed his stomach and doubled over. Sally stepped to the side, firmly grasped the broomstick with both hands, and swung it hard. She finished him off with a blow to the head, and he fell to the ground.

Stanley was hiding in the toy department. He concealed himself behind a display of Princess Cathleen dolls. The man chasing him walked by, and Stanley relaxed. He leaned into the display and accidentally activated a doll.

"I say, would you like a spot of tea?" the doll asked.

The man turned toward the display while Stanley fumbled to turn the doll off. The man walked to the display and stared at Stanley, who seemed to be playing with the doll. For some reason Stanley was more embarrassed than scared.

"It's not what you think," Stanley said with a weak smile, holding up the doll. "I'm not playing with this doll."

"I love you," the doll said, and Stanley nervously laughed.

The man with the sunglasses didn't care what Stanley was doing. He reached to grab Stanley. Stanley finally got his emotions in the proper order.

"Aaaahhh!" Stanley screamed.

Gonggggg!

Beth Ann smashed the man in the side of the head with the powder can. His sunglasses flew off, and he rubbed the side of his head. He turned to Beth Ann with his red eyes focused on her. As he walked forward, Sally whacked him on the other side of the head with the broomstick. He fell over the Princess Cathleen display, and the boxes of dolls covered him. The commotion activated some dolls.

"It is so nice to see you."

"I say, would you like a spot of tea?"

"I love you. I love you-you-you. Love-love you. Eeeerhhh," a doll said and went silent.

All of her friends gathered around Sally, including Horace and his partner.

"Let's go!" Sally yelled. "I know a way out."

Everyone followed Sally as she ran to the "Employees Only" door. When they were all at the door, they looked around. More

Goblin King followers were converging on them from different departments of the store.

"Come on," Sally said and opened the metal door. They all ran through. When they were all in, Sally slammed the door and slid a bolt over to lock it. She immediately turned around and hugged Horace.

"Oh, Horace, I missed you," she said. "What's happening?"

"This is a very dangerous situation, Sally," he said. "The Goblin King is attacking your world."

"Who?" Sally asked.

"We're doomed," Stanley moaned.

"Shut up," Beth Ann said, poking him in the ribs with her elbow.

"I'll explain later. This is Hector, my apprentice," Horace said, pointing at the blond-haired elf.

Hector nodded at Sally and held his hand out. "I'm honored," he said. "I've heard a lot about you, Sally."

Sally shook his hand and introduced her friends. "These are my friends, Beth Ann, Stanley, Rodney, and Sammy," she said, pointing to each as she named them.

Boom. Boom. Boom. Something heavy was hitting the metal door.

"We have to go," Horace said, turning to Sally. "We've been here before. I think you know the way out."

Sally led the way, and they ran down the different levels on the metal stairs. Horace stayed right behind Sally, and Hector guarded the rear. They reached the bottom of the stairs and stood before the large gray metal door. Horace opened it, and they all ran into the Somers Department Store warehouse. It was unusually silent; no one seemed to be around. They ran down the aisles with high metal racks filled with merchandise on wooden pallets. They ran through the large warehouse, toward the exit. They reached an open area where steel-wheeled tracks were used to load the trucks that pulled into the bay doors of the warehouse.

They heard the sound of the engine and smelled the natural gas before they saw anything. From a side aisle a large green forklift truck turned a corner to their left and raced toward them with its engine revving. A man driving the forklift tried to run them down, and they all scattered. The forklift truck skidded to a stop, and the smell of burning rubber mixed with the propane. The man switched gears and jammed his foot down on the accelerator. The wheels spun on the concrete floor, and the forklift shot into reverse, toward Stanley, who had jumped into a box of towels on a pallet on a floor-level rack. Stanley ducked into the box when he saw the machine coming at him. The truck smashed into the metal rack, which bent but did not break. The back end of the forklift was able to hit part of the box before being stopped, and the front of the box crumpled over Stanley.

Horace grabbed the handle of a manual forklift. He pointed the front wheels forward and stood behind them on the forks. Still holding the handle, he used his right leg to propel the forklift forward like you would a scooter and rolled toward the steel-wheeled tracks. He picked up speed, put both feet on the forks, glided, and waited for the right moment. He jumped high onto the tracks just before the forklift crashed into the frame. Horace surfed the steel-wheeled tracks and leapt onto the forks of the truck that was trying to harm his friends. The red-eyed operator turned away from Stanley and stared at Horace. He used the hand-operated controls to raise the forks. Horace balanced on the forks and did not fall off. The driver shifted the gears, rolled forward, turned the forklift toward a cinder block wall, gunned the engine, and drove straight at it.

"Horace!" Sally yelled.

Horace turned to the wall and then forward. He quickly calculated his options and jumped from the forks to the top of the safety cage that surrounded the driver. Moving to the passenger side, he grabbed the tubular bar that held up the cage, swung into the cab, and kicked the driver out of the forklift. It slowed to a halt as Horace took the controls.

Everyone gathered around Stanley's crumpled box while Horace drove over. He lowered the forks as he drove. With grim faces Sally and Beth Ann pulled open the front end of box. Everyone was relieved when Stanley popped his head up.

"Am I alive?" he asked touching his head.

Everyone laughed as Sally and Beth Ann grabbed an arm and helped him out of the box.

"Everyone on!" Horace yelled.

They all crammed into the cab of the forklift. It was a tight fit, and bodies and faces were squeezed together. Stanley was smashed next to Beth Ann; their faces almost touched. Neither could move their arms, but Stanley smiled and puckered his lips for a kiss.

"Don't you dare, Stanley," Beth Ann said angrily. "I will bite you."

Stanley stopped immediately. "Just joking," he said meekly.

Horace pressed down on the gas. The wheels spun, and the forklift lurched forward. They reached the end of the warehouse. A large number of red-eyed employees were waiting for them.

"Hold on!" Horace yelled.

He made a left turn, and employees jumped out of the way. Horace raised the forks and drove toward a large wooden side door. The forklift truck reached maximum speed.

"Aaaaaggghhh!" Sally and her friends screamed.

Horace crashed through, splintering the door. He drove the forklift out of the warehouse yard and onto the street.

"Take a right and head for the school," Sally said.

Horace turned right and pressed the accelerator to the floor.

They passed a line of public buses that were parked in front of the mall. The Goblin King was directing all of the red-eyed adults onto the buses for a trip to the candy factory. He was now in his own body, wearing his black trench coat and holding Miss Mephisto. There was no longer any need for deceit. He watched Horace and his friends scoot by in the forklift. He pressed his lips together in anger for a moment and then relaxed by taking deep breaths.

"This has been more difficult than I thought," he said, stroking Miss Mephisto. "All great leaders must have patience when dealing with adversity. Time and planning are on my side." He turned and yelled at Seymour, "Get everyone on the buses quickly!"

"Yeck. Yeck," Seymour said and started to poke the adults with a sharp stick to move them more quickly.

CHAPTER 7

Back to School

They rolled down the street in the forklift and turned down the boulevard leading to the school. The industrial machine did not provide the comfy ride of a passenger car. The forklift truck bounced up and down while the forks shook and rattled around. The jam-packed passengers were jostled about. The big engine vibrated the entire truck and the occupants' bones.

"Weeahhh. Weeahh. Whoop. Whoop. Whoop."

They all heard the noise behind them, but only Sally could turn her head a bit to look around. Officer MacNamara, the former special forces soldier, was following them in his police cruiser and waving them over.

"Pull over, Horace," Sally said. "It's officer MacNamara. You know him. He's a good guy."

"We can't trust anyone right now," Horace said.

Horace continued to drive, but the forklift started to sputter and jerk. They were running out of propane. Horace pulled over to the side of the road, and the forklift truck came to a halt. With one final sputter, shake, and backfire, the engine cut off.

Officer MacNamara glided up behind them and stopped. He turned his engine off and stepped out of his cruiser. He was still lean and calm, but everyone sensed that he was capable of controlled, efficient violence. He was wearing the same dark sunglasses he always wore.

With extreme effort and much pulling, pushing, and twisting everyone got out of the forklift. "Aahhh," Stanley said, holding his right leg and falling to the ground. "My leg's asleep," he said, rolling on the grass and rubbing his leg to regain circulation. Sally and her friends jumped up and down and squeezed their hands open and closed to wake their limbs up. Stanley recovered and stood up. When they were through, Officer MacNamara walked closer and waved them to come forward.

"Come with me. I'll drive you to a safe location," he said.

"Let's go," Sally said, stepping forward, but Horace grabbed her arm and shook his head with a stern look.

Officer MacNamara walked closer and smiled.

"Who am I?" Sally asked Officer MacNamara.

He didn't answer, and Sally became concerned. He was almost upon her. Sally reached up quickly and knocked his sunglasses up. His red eyes blazed brightly.

"Run!" Sally yelled.

"Freeze!" Officer MacNamara yelled, pulling out his gun and pointing it at Sally.

Everyone froze.

"Don't kill me please," Stanley said, raising his hands straight up into the air.

"Easy man," Rodney said, putting his hands out.

"What are you—loco?" Sammy said.

Beth Ann crossed her arms over her chest. "What are you going to do?" she asked angrily. "Shoot a bunch of kids?"

"Everyone in the car," he said, waving them forward with his left hand and pointing the gun with his right. "Nice and easy."

Horace and Hector tensed their bodies and prepared for action. Horace glanced at Hector and nodded. They were ready to attack this possessed cop. Officer MacNamara turned around quickly when he heard his cruiser's engine start. The wheels squealed, and the car pulled out. It roared toward Officer MacNamara. Everyone screamed and ran behind the forklift for protection. When he was safely behind the truck, Stanley fainted and collapsed. Officer MacNamara raised his gun to fire at the fast-approaching vehicle. He squeezed off one round, and it smashed through the windshield on the driver's side but did not stop the car. Officer MacNamara jumped out of the way, rolling down a grassy embankment on the side of the road. His gun flew out of his hand as he rolled. The police cruiser screeched to a halt in front of the forklift. The door opened. A small boy with a thin face, brown eyes, and long brown-and-black streaked hair poked his head out. He was wearing khaki overalls with a white undershirt and a straw farmer's hat.

"Get in," he yelled.

Sally revived Stanley and helped him to his feet. She noticed that his nose had been running even when he was unconscious. They all ran to the car. The boy reached over and opened the front passenger door. Sally, Horace, and Hector jumped in. Beth Ann couldn't open the rear door. Hector leaned over the front seat and opened the door. Beth Ann reached in, grabbed a box of chocolates off the backseat, and threw them on the road.

Beth Ann, Sammy, Rodney, and Stanley got in, shuffled over, and bunched together. All doors were slammed, and the boy put the car in gear, punched his foot down on the accelerator, and pulled away quickly. He turned to Sally and smiled. He had small, sharp, crooked teeth. He turned his eyes back to the road. He sat on the edge of the front seat so his feet could reach the pedals and stretched up to look over the steering wheel. Sally looked in the rearview mirror and watched Officer

MacNamara climb out of the ditch. He stood in the middle of the road and watched them drive away.

"Who are you?" Sally asked the boy.

"I'm Seth," he said with a smile. "Glad to meet you."

He held out his hand, and Sally gave it a quick shake.

"Bad time at the mall," the boy said. "My parents are red-eyed slaves. Does anyone know what's happening?"

"The Goblin King has attacked," Horace replied and studied the boy closely.

"Who is that?" Seth asked.

"He is an evil ruler from another world in another dimension of space and time," Horace said slowly. "I've encountered him before, and I'm afraid that this is really an attack against me."

"Wow. That's crazy," Seth said while everyone else sat in silence. "What do we do now?"

"To the school," Sally said. "Hopefully, everyone will meet up with us there."

"Which way?" Seth asked.

Sally looked at him suspiciously.

"I'm not from around here," Seth said. "I grew up on a farm. That's how I know how to drive. I've been driving the family truck and tractor for years."

"Go straight," Sally said. "I'll tell you when to turn."

Seth drove straight down the busiest main road in Somertown, but there was no traffic. They were in the only car that was moving. Sally turned to Horace.

"Are you all right? How bad are things? I haven't heard you rhyme. That is not a good sign," she said with a smile.

Everyone looked at Horace and waited for his reply.

"I'm fine. There will be plenty of time for rhyme," Horace said with a small smile. He stopped smiling and became serious. "Right now things are pretty bad. The Goblin King has the initiative with a surprise attack. He has made gains. We have to regroup and plan."

They drove awhile in silence. Everyone was thinking about what Horace had said. Sally looked out the front window and became very confused. "What is that?" she asked, and everyone popped their heads up and looked out.

Something odd was on the side of the road. Jackie Chambers, the heaviest kid in Sally's class, was dressed as Friar Tuck, one of Robin Hood's Merry Men, and sitting by the side of the road. Jackie had lost some weight, but he was still big and round and weighed over two hundred pounds. His brown hair, as usual, was cut the same length around his entire head and was now perfect for his costume. This was odd in itself, but something else grabbed everyone's attention. Everyone was curious and wanted to know the answer to the same question: Why was Jackie Chambers sitting on top of a man?

Seth slowed down, and everyone stared. He pulled the car to the side of the road, slowly rolled up to Jackie, and stopped. Hector opened the passenger-side window. Jackie was sitting on the man's chest, and the full force of his two hundred-plus pounds was causing the man to moan in great distress.

"Jackie, what are you doing?" Sally asked.

"Hi, Sally," he said with a smile. "This crazy guy keeps following me and trying to make me eat that poison chocolate. I saw what it did to Corey. This guy and his friends were going from house to house in the neighborhood."

Everyone got out of the car and walked over for a closer look-see. The man had his eyes closed and was still moaning.

"I've been fighting with this guy for a mile. This is the only way I could get some rest. He's like an annoying gnat," Jackie said.

"Are his eyes red?" Sally asked.

"You bet," Jackie replied. "Like a devil dog. Do you want to see them?"

"Yes," Sally said.

Jackie pinched the man in the stomach and gave it a little twist.

"Aaaahhh!" the man screamed and opened his eyes. They were indeed red.

"Get in the car and come with us," Sally said. "We're going to the school."

"Okay," Jackie said with a smile. "This is getting a little boring."

He stood up, grabbed the man by his arms, and lifted him to his feet. The sneaky codger reached into his pocket and pulled out a piece of candy. Jackie cuffed him across the head and sent him reeling down the embankment. He eventually fell to the ground, and chocolate candies poured out of his pockets and tumbled about as he rolled down the hill.

They got back into the car before the determined man could compose himself. Jackie was the last to get in. He looked to the front door, and Hector slammed it shut. Jackie started to squeeze into the backseat.

"Hector, let him in the front. There's more room," Rodney said.

"Deuna angla," Hector said, pretending not to understand Rodney. He and Horace looked at each other and smiled.

"In Elfin that means 'I don't understand English,'" Horace whispered in Sally's ear.

"Excuse me," Jackie said, pressing against Stanley with his great bulk. "Scusey."

"Aaahh, come on," Stanley said.

Everyone in the backseat, already sitting tightly together, was squeezed even tighter by Jackie's steady and inevitable entry into the car. Like a slow-moving flabby ice floe, he was a force of nature that could not be repelled. The pressure caused Beth Ann to pop up off the seat first, and she sat on Stanley's lap. Sammy was next, and he sat on Rodney's lap. Jackie squirmed around to get comfortable, and everyone else was jostled and squeezed. Beth Ann's head fell against the backseat. She turned her head and stared directly into Stanley's face.

"Hello," Stanley said, smiling. "We meet again."

"Shut up, Stanley," she said. She sat up, repositioned herself on Stanley's lap, and leaned back, pressing the top of her back and shoulder into Stanley's face. Stanley turned his smashed face to the side so he could breathe. "Okay, I'm sorry. I'm sorry," he pleaded. Beth Ann sat forward and relieved the pressure from Stanley's head. "That's better," she said while Rodney and Sammy chuckled.

"Jackie, my man," Rodney said. "You have got to go on a diet."

"I have lost some weight," Jackie said. "I've been eating healthy and exercising. Didn't you notice that I've slimmed down?"

Sammy looked at Rodney, and they both shook their heads.

"Yeah, I noticed," Sammy said. "You're looking good."

"Thanks," Jackie said and smiled.

"Buckle up and let's go," Sally said.

When everyone was secure, Seth hit the gas, and the car lurched forward.

CHAPTER 8

EVIL ON THE WING

The Goblin King walked into the manufacturing area of the candy factory. He was carrying his black pouch.

"Faster," he yelled at the red-eyed employees, who were already working hard.

The conveyor belts moved faster, and the employees had to keep pace. The factory was at full capacity; it had never produced this much chocolate. The Goblin King walked to the chocolate vats and poured more black powder from his pouch into each one. The black smoke had thinned but now grew thicker and billowed out of the vats, rose up to the ceiling, flowed through the large ventilator fans, and poured out into Somertown's atmosphere. It grew into a large cloud over the factory and then started moving with the wind. Gobs of black-and-brown gunk flowed out of discharge pipes and into a river next to the factory. The river flowed to streams and eventually to the Somertown Lake, which supplied the water for the town. The sludge from the factory quickly discolored the river. The original circle of evil waste grew larger, and the river began to have the consistency of a black gooey swamp.

The Goblin King walked up the stairs to the factory office. He looked out of the window and gazed at the polluted river and the now-giant cloud of moving black smoke. He was pleased with himself and smiled.

The black cloud moved to the center of Somertown. Sally watched the cloud move over the sun. It became darker, and the sun became bright orange as it tried to shine through the black haze.

"What's that?" she asked Horace and pointed to the cloud.

"It looks like a spell," he replied. "It could do anything."

"We better get to the school," Stanley said.

"Wait. Turn here!" Sally said to Seth. "I want to pick something up at my house."

Seth turned the car, and they drove to Sally's house. The car stopped, and Sally jumped out with Horace and Hector. Baron Von Muncher came running. He jumped into Horace's arms, knocked him over, and licked his face.

"Stop. Stop. This is over the top," Horace said, laughing.

Horace stood up and petted Von Muncher on the head. Sally unhooked the heavy chain from Von Muncher's collar. She gathered it up by looping it over the palm of her left hand.

"He remembers you," Sally said, smiling.

"And me he," Horace said.

Sally opened the back door of the car. All of her friends screamed "No" and Baron Von Muncher excitedly jumped in. He scrambled onto Jackie's ample lap and stared at Stanley. Von Muncher was panting and drooling.

"Oh, no," Stanley moaned.

Beth Ann was able to lean away, but Stanley's arms were pinned. He couldn't move when Von Muncher decided to lick his face with his long, thick slobbery tongue.

"Ewwww," Stanley said while everyone else laughed.

Sally walked to the car with Baron Von Muncher's long chain. She handed it to Hector. She closed the back door, and when everyone was safely in the car, they continued their journey to the school.

The growing dark cloud eclipsed the sun, and it looked like twilight on this sunny day. It slowly drifted over Saint

Bartholomew's Orphanage and lingered. Slowly at first and then more quickly, the stone gargoyles that surrounded the top of the old orphanage began to come to life. Their rock-hard features began to soften, their petrified limbs moved, and their wings unfurled after decades of stillness. The gargoyles were not identical. Some had big noses, some had big ears, some had dopey faces, some looked mean, and some looked happy. Some had tails whereas others did not. They retained the same look and demeanor as the masons had intended when they were carved from the hard stone. They all had sharp teeth but differed in color. There were different tones of green and purple as well as those that retained their original stone color. They also had different eye colors. Some had red, some green, some yellow, some blue, some black, and some had one eye that was a different color than the other.

    They leapt from their high perches and took flight. Dozens gathered with their brethren in mid-air. They seemed to be discussing a course of action. After a moment the tightly packed formation broke apart, and the gargoyles attacked the orphanage. They smashed into windows and carried off unsuspecting children and adults. The gargoyles did not seem bothered by their victims' screams and cries. The sounds of the agony subsided with distance as the winged creatures flew swiftly toward the candy factory.

CHAPTER 9

School's in Session— The Battle Begins

Sally and her crew pulled up to the maroon metal double front doors of her school. Sally's message had been passed on, and a large group of kids were gathered there. The children made it back to the school quickly. Moving at a brisk pace, they could travel the distance from mall to school faster than a car. They were not slowed down by a government-planned road system. They cut through open fields, forests, and playgrounds. They hopped fences, scurried between homes—and even through homes. They followed secret routes that only the school kids knew. Old shortcuts were passed on from older students to younger, but new ones were created each year. Many of the kids had shed their bulky costumes for the journey. Sally noticed that the Lunch Box Boy and his little siblings were huddled together and costume-free.

Sally and her friends got out of the squad car and approached them. Everyone heard a faint screeching and looked up to the sky. In the distance a large flock of gargoyles was quickly approaching. Some veered off toward the town whereas others flew directly toward the school.

"Sally, is there a big room where you can take everyone?" Horace asked.

"The gym," Sally replied.

SCHOOL'S IN SESSION—THE BATTLE BEGINS

"Take everyone to the gym and lock all the doors," Horace said. "Hector, you go to warn the people in town."

"Okay, nice and calm," Sally said loudly. "Let's go to the gym. Like a fire drill."

Sally gathered the kids together, and they all lined up. Beth Ann and Stanley opened each side of the large metal maroon doors, which opened inward. Stanley's side kept swinging shut on its own. He saw a doorstop on the floor and kicked the wooden wedge under the door to hold it in place. Sally and her friends then marched the kids through the front doors of the school.

Horace and Hector ran to Officer MacNamara's police cruiser. Horace grabbed the officer's official issue riot baton, and Hector took Baron Von Muncher's long chain. They ran to the front doors and took their positions. Baron Von Muncher sat between them.

The gargoyles started their descent just as the last little boy was into the school. Sally closed one side of the double doors. She looked up and saw a gargoyle swooping down at the open door. She quickly tried to slam the remaining door closed, but it was stuck. Sally screamed when the gargoyle was close. Horace perfectly timed his jump. He leaped into the air and clubbed the sneering gargoyle on the head. This mighty blow sent the gargoyle careening and smashing into the wall of the school. Horace turned to fight as more gargoyles dropped from the sky like winged guided missiles.

Sally tried to close the door, but it was jammed. The doorstop was wedged securely under the door, and she could not kick it free. Horace continued to jump and club while Hector swung the chain over his head. The chain whipped the intruders and drove them away. Baron Von Muncher was growling, baring his teeth, and snapping at the evil flock. The three combatants were effectively holding the defensive line.

Sally kept pulling and pushing the door and to her relief it started to budge. Her efforts moved the doorstop a little at a time. The unconscious gargoyle that had smashed into the wall began to move. It slowly crawled to the door. Sally saw it and desperately tried to pull and push the door. The purplish gargoyle had large pointed ears, a sharp nose, long chin with a chip off the bottom, sharp teeth, and evil black eyes. Crawling forward, it looked like a giant flying lizard with its tail waving in the air. It hissed as it moved forward.

She had to remove that stuck doorstop quickly. She finally managed to get enough of it out so that she could kick it away. She slammed the door closed, but the gargoyle grabbed it with one of its clawed hands before it was fully closed. She braced her body against the door and stared with wide eyes at the human-like hand with its gray and purple scales, long fingers, and sharp claws. That one hand was in the school and was now trying to push the door open.

"Beth Ann!" Sally screamed.

Beth Ann ran down the school corridor to the front door.

"What?" she asked.

"That!" Sally said, nodding at the scaly hand with wide-opened eyes.

"Aaaaaggghhh!" Beth Ann screamed. She quickly picked up the wooden doorstop and started maniacally chopping at the offending hand.

The gargoyle made a deep growling moan and scratched at the front of the door with its other hand. It smashed the door with its shoulder, and the door bounced open a bit. Sally was thrown back by the force and then leaned against the door to hold it shut. She was trying hard, but the gargoyle's lunges were very powerful. She was losing the battle; the door was inching open. Beth Ann joined her in leaning against the door.

"Keep pushing!" Sally desperately cried out.

After each lunge Beth Ann would smash the gargoyle's hand with the doorstop. She grunted with each blow like a tennis player hitting a hard backhand. Each time the gargoyle would shriek and then hit the door again. The girls were tiring, and the door was opening wider. The gargoyle smiled because the opening was almost wide enough to squeeze its body into the school. As its head poked into the school, drool dripped from its mouth. Sally and Beth Ann screamed and pushed, but they knew they were in danger. The gargoyle had seized the momentum and pushed with renewed energy.

The gargoyle felt a tapping on its back. It pulled its head out and turned. Horace was tapping it on the back with his stick. The gargoyle's eyes saddened, and it moaned lowly. Horace whacked it on the head, and it screeched, let go of the door, ran a few steps, and flew away, holding its head. Sally slammed the door fully closed, and Beth Ann locked it with the turning of a knob that bolted both sides together.

Some gargoyles had retreated in pain, but others were still attacking. When Hector swung his chain at one with a big round dopey face, it wrapped around its neck. Hector swung up and landed on the back of the shocked gargoyle. It tried to flap its wings, buck back, and throw Hector off. Hector pulled the chain tight, and the gargoyle gave up. Hector rode the gargoyle like a flying horse. He used the chain to guide the gargoyle's head, kicked its thighs with his heels, and flew toward town. Horace and Baron Von Muncher watched him fly high and away.

CHAPTER 10

SOMERTOWN IS WARNED

Hector flew through the streets of Somertown and shouted a warning. From the sky he could see gargoyles scampering and hopping on foot in the neighborhood. They were hunched over when they moved and carried bags of candy. They were going from door to door, seeking victims. They had also set up a stand on the street with a sign offering free candy and were laying bagfuls on porches and doorsteps.

Hector was too late to warn some folks who had been ganged up on and forced to eat candy. Their eyes were red, and they slowly walked down the streets and made their way to a bus parked on a main street.

"Stay in your homes and lock your doors!" he kept repeating. "Don't eat any candy!"

The people in the neighborhood were frightened, but they heeded the warning. A thin old woman with white hair and a kind face pushed her window down and locked it. She was wearing a white nightgown and blue fuzzy slippers. She walked to the front door and saw the doorknob turning.

"Oh, my!" she said.

A nasty little gargoyle formed an evil smile with its sharp pointy teeth when the door creaked open. It laughed with a hissing sound. It slowly opened the door a few inches, put one of its clawed feet in, and peeked through the crack. Its eyes glanced to the left and widened when it saw the dainty old woman swing a hammer down hard on its foot.

"EEEEEakkkkk!" the gargoyle screamed and threw its bag of candy on the porch.

It hobbled off the porch and moaned every time its painful foot touched the ground. It ran a few steps, limping and moaning, and flew away, rubbing its painful foot.

"That will teach him not to come into my house without an invitation," she said to herself with a little smile.

She put the hammer down on a small table and locked the door. She sat in her rocking chair and picked up the book she had been reading before she was so rudely interrupted. She found her page, smiled, rocked slowly, and continued reading.

Hector looked down and saw a cute young girl standing under a tree. A gargoyle was swooping down toward her. Hector pulled the chain around the gargoyle's neck and flew to save the girl.

The gargoyle landed in front of the girl. It hunched over with outstretched arms, hissed, and bared its formidable fangs. The girl did not seem to be afraid of this dangerous creature. The gargoyle stepped forward. Hector was worried that he would be too late. The girl retreated, dragging her feet through the fallen leaves and pressing her back against the trunk of the tree. The gargoyle stepped forward again. In an instant the startled gargoyle fell to the ground and was pulled along and over the leaves. The gargoyle's left ankle was caught in a rope snare. A group of boys and girls appeared from behind another tree and were pulling on the rope and cheering wildly. The young girl ran and joined her friends in the celebration. The rope was looped over a tree branch. They stopped pulling when the gargoyle was upside down and swinging in the air.

Hector laughed at this clever trap and yelled out a warning: "Great work—but you have to stay indoors until it is safe. There will be others."

"Okay," the young girl who had lured the gargoyle said.

The children tied the rope to a fencepost and left the gargoyle dangling. They heeded Hector's warning and ran to their homes. The hapless gargoyle made a high-pitched bird-like screech calling for aid.

Hector flew high in the air and looked around in all directions. He smiled when he saw a large pack of neighborhood dogs attacking the gargoyles and protecting their human friends. Mongrels and purebred dogs of all shapes and sizes were working together. Mastiffs, poodles, terriers, and tiny lapdogs patrolled and fought tirelessly for their owners, neighbors, and friends. The gargoyles launched into the air as the dogs nipped at their rears. Some gargoyles escaped, but others shrieked when the snapping bites hit the intended target.

Hector turned and saw a large number of gargoyles converging around Saint Bartholomew's Orphanage. He pulled on the gargoyle's chain and flew in that direction.

Sister Mary Worthington, the petite superintendent of the orphanage and a great friend of Horace, was hiding in Saint Bartholomew's Chapel with a large group of children she was able to save and protect. She heard a noise and looked around. She was unaware that a window had been left partially open at the back of the chapel. She ran back and was horrified to see that an ugly green gargoyle with a pitted and chipped face was trying to climb through the window.

"You devil!" she screamed.

The gargoyle looked up at her with its head and arms sticking through the window and snarled. Sister Mary produced a yardstick from under her robe and started to ruthlessly pummel the gargoyle about the head, neck, and arms. She was thin but surprisingly strong and quick. The lightning fast blows rained down, and the speed and power of each blow only grew in intensity. The children heard the swishing and thwacking and thought that a small helicopter had entered the chapel.

SOMERTOWN IS WARNED

"EEEEackkk!" the gargoyle kept screaming.

The gargoyle fell out of the window but grabbed onto the sill. Sister Mary slammed the window down on its clawed hands. She heard the screams, waited a moment, and opened the window. The gargoyle released its grip, pushed off from the side of the building with its feet, and flew away whimpering. Sister Mary slammed the window shut and locked it.

Sister Mary stood in front of the window. She breathed slowly and deeply for a moment and tried to relax. She heard a noise and quickly turned her head and stared at the chapel door, which started to open. She ran to the door but could hardly see in the dark room. The door opened, and she swung her yardstick at the small figure standing in the dark. The figure moved quickly and grabbed the stick before it hit.

"I'm a friend of Horace, and I'm here to help," Hector said as he relaxed his grip on the yardstick.

"Thank God," Sister Mary said, bringing the yardstick down to her side.

Hector moved into the light and smiled at Sister Mary.

"You must be Sister Mary. Horace told me about you with great admiration. My name is Hector," he said, holding his hand out.

Sister Mary put the yardstick on a table and shook his hand.

"Come in, young one," she said with a smile.

Sister Mary relaxed and so did the children when they saw this beautiful young elf. Then they screamed when the chapel door was violently thrown open. Percival Strickland, the gigantic disciplinarian at the orphanage, stood in the doorway with his red eyes visible in the darkness.

He caught Hector by surprise and struck him with a heavy blow that sent him crashing into the wall. The big man moved quickly. Hector had crumpled to the floor in a daze.

Mr. Strickland grabbed him by the neck, lifted him high, and slammed his back against the wall. He shuffled his feet to the right and slid Hector along the wall until they reached the chapel pews. Mr. Strickland braced his feet against the base of the pew, put both hands around Hector's neck, and leaned in with all his great weight. Hector could not breathe. He grabbed Mr. Strickland's hands, but he could not pull them away from his neck.

Thwaaack!

Sister Mary was standing on the seat of the pew that Mr. Strickland was using to brace his feet. She had hit him on the head with her large family bible that she held firmly with both hands. This book contained both the Old and New Testaments. She kept it in the chapel so that it would always be handy and others could use it. Mr. Strickland reeled sideways and shook his head. He was still holding Hector by the neck in midair, but his grip had loosened. Hector kicked him in the stomach.

"Aaaahhh," he growled. He then lowered Hector and turned toward Sister Mary.

Thwaaack! Sister Mary nailed him with a second powerful shot to the jaw.

Mr. Strickland's head whipped to the side, his eyes closed, and his knees buckled. His grip loosened, and Hector fell to the floor. Hector grabbed his arm and threw the big man over his shoulder. Mr. Strickland flew in the air, and his back landed on the floor with a great thud that vibrated the candlestick holders at the back of the chapel, and the candle flames waved and flickered. As he opened his eyes, Hector stood on his chest, looking down. Mr. Strickland saw the punch coming, but it was too fast for him to avoid. Hector knocked him out with one sharp, powerful blow to the jaw. The kids cheered.

Two gargoyles were in the doorway, and they witnessed this show of force. They looked at Sister Mary, who was still holding her lethal bible. They turned to Hector, who glared at them. Hector made two fists and jumped off of Mr. Strickland's chest. The gargoyles looked at each other and ran away.

CHAPTER 11

THE SCHOOL IS BREACHED

Horace and Baron Von Muncher successfully defended the entrance to the school. The gargoyles could not defeat them. Some were bloodied from Von Muncher's bites, and some lay unconscious from Horace's stick. Horace and the Baron stood together and waited for another charge.

Sally and her friends finished getting all of the kids comfortably settled in the gym. Sally stood at the door to the gym, looking down the corridor. It was well lit because Jackie had found the electric utility room and turned every light in the school on.

"I'm going to help Horace," she said.

"I don't think that is a good idea," Stanley said nervously and wiped his nose with his handkerchief.

"Stanley's right," Beth Ann said. "I think Horace would want us to stay here."

"But Horace and Von Muncher might need some help," Rodney said.

"Wouldn't hurt to check," Sammy said.

"We should all stay here," Seth said.

Jackie Chambers didn't say anything because he was eating a candy bar he had produced from some secret place. Sally thought for a moment.

"Seth, we're going to check on them. You and Jackie stay here and watch everyone. Keep this door locked," she said, pointing at the gym doors.

"Okay," Seth said while Jackie chewed on his candy bar and nodded his head in agreement.

Sally and her friends walked out of the gym and into the corridor. The gym doors were identical to the front doors except that they opened outward. Seth and Jackie closed the doors, and Sally heard the bolt lock them out. They walked down the corridor toward the front entrance.

The gargoyles were beaten. They flew up into the air and huddled closely together. They seemed to be talking to each other.

"I don't like this," Horace said to the Baron, who howled in response.

"I agree," Horace said.

The gargoyles flew down again but turned left and flew over the heads of Horace and the Baron. They crashed through different windows on the side of the building and tumbled into desks and rolled on the floor of the classrooms with glass sprinkling everywhere. They had breached the school's defenses, and the kids were at risk.

They all heard the explosion of windows and stood still in the corridor.

"What was that?" Stanley asked in a scared whisper.

"I don't know," Sally said. "Be quiet."

They lowered their heads and turned their ears in the direction of the noise. They then heard the clack, clack, clack of claws on hard linoleum. A group of gargoyles turned a corner at the opposite end of the corridor from Sally and her friends. The two groups were surprised and stared at each other for a long moment.

"Run!" Sally yelled. "Try to make your way back to the gym."

Everyone bolted, and the gargoyles followed. Rodney and Sammy froze for a moment.

"Let's roll," Rodney said.

"I'm with you," Sammy said.

When they reached the end of the corridor, Sally turned left while Beth Ann and Stanley turned right. They ran in opposite directions in the new corridor. Sally and her friends had the home-field advantage over the gargoyles. They had memorized every twist and turn of the maze of corridors in the large school. Rodney and Sammy reached the intersection and turned in the same direction as Sally. The gargoyles reached the intersection and stopped. They looked in both directions, but their prey had disappeared. They split up and went in both directions. The clacking from their hopping and walking echoed in the hallway lined with classroom doors. They each picked a door, opened it, and hopped in to investigate.

THE FINAL CURTAIN CLOSES

Beth Ann and Stanley ran into the auditorium and hid behind some props on the stage. They knelt behind a wooden desk and looked at each other.

"What are we going to do?" Stanley asked in a whisper.

"I don't know," Beth Ann replied, holding her finger to her lips. "Be quiet."

They heard the door to the auditorium creak open, and they ducked down. They heard the door close.

A gargoyle walked down the steps of the auditorium. The red carpet on the steps allowed him to walk in silence. The auditorium doubled as a theater, and the school's plays and shows were presented here. The stadium style seating sloped down to the stage. The gargoyle looked down the first few rows of seats that it passed and stopped. It pushed one of the self-retracting seats down. It ran its clawed hand over the comfortable red fabric and smiled. It sat down, crossed its legs, and leaned back to relax.

"Aaahhh," it said.

The stone-colored gargoyle had large floppy ears, droopy eyes, and a hooked nose. It had a perpetual silly smile and did not look overly intelligent.

Beth Ann peeked up from behind the desk and then ducked back down.

"Is one up there?" Stanley whispered.

"Yes," she replied.

"What's it doing?" he asked.

"I think it's taking a nap," Beth Ann said.

"That's crazy," Stanley said. "You must be seeing things."

Beth Ann punched him in the arm.

"Owwww," Stanley said quietly and rubbed his arm.

The gargoyle looked down at the orchestra pit in front of the stage and leaned forward. It put both of its hands in the air and began to wave them back and forth. Stanley peeked over the desk and then sat back down.

"What's it doing?" Beth Ann asked.

"I think it's pretending to conduct an orchestra," he said. Beth Ann punched him in the arm again with an angry look.

"Owwww," Stanley said and rubbed his arm again.

"Don't play around with me, Stanley. This is not the time," she said.

"I'm not," Stanley quietly whined.

Beth Ann quickly poked her head up and sat back down.

"I'm sorry," she said without looking at Stanley.

"I told you," Stanley said.

Stanley shifted his body over a bit to get comfortable and banged his elbow on the desk drawer. His elbow hit hard, making a loud banging noise.

"Owww," Stanley said, rubbing his elbow. "My funny bone."

The acoustics were good in the auditorium, and the sound carried well to the back row. The gargoyle heard the noise with its sharp hearing from its oversized ears and stopped conducting. It leaned its neck forward and stared directly at the desk. It then turned its head toward the stage and cupped its ear. The gargoyle quickly jumped out of its seat and onto the steps. It flapped its wings and flew to the stage.

It landed on the stage, with its clawed feet clacking on the wooden floor and its tail swaying back and forth as it walked. It examined an umbrella that was in an umbrella stand by the left wing of the stage. The gargoyle pulled it out and ran its hands over the black umbrella. It shot open. "Eeeeeeckkk!" the gargoyle screeched in fear and surprise and threw the umbrella. The opened umbrella hit the shade of a floor lamp, and both crashed to the ground. Beth Ann started to scream and then clamped both hands over her mouth. The gargoyle turned and stared at the desk.

The gargoyle walked across the stage. Beth Ann's and Stanley's eyes widened as they heard the clacking feet get closer and closer. They stared at each other for a moment. The gargoyle was surprised again when Beth Ann jumped up. She grabbed a gun that was lying on the desk and pointed it at the gargoyle.

"Hold it right there," she said.

The gargoyle trembled and moaned and put both arms up in the air. Stanley crawled to the side of the stage and hid behind a curtain. The gargoyle stared and examined the gun for a moment. It then cocked its head to one side and took a step forward.

"Bang!" the gun erupted loudly when she pulled the trigger and shot at the ceiling. White smoke puffed from the barrel. She pointed the gun back at the gargoyle.

"The next one's for you!" she yelled. "Leave before it's too late."

The gargoyle looked up at the ceiling. It did not hear an impact and could not see any damage. It crinkled its nose and tilted its head back as it sniffed the air for gunpowder. It thought for a moment and then smiled when it reached a conclusion. It took another step forward.

Bang! Beth Ann shot again, and the gargoyle stopped. It held its stomach where the gun had been pointing. It slowly looked down and pulled its hands away. There was no damage.

"Harok, harok, harok," the gargoyle laughed. It doubled over, held its belly, and slapped its thigh with its hand. It stood up straight and waved its clawed index finger at Beth Ann. It then began to move forward. Beth Ann threw the heavy fake gun, which hit the gargoyle in the head.

"Aagah, aagah!" the gargoyle cried out and held its sore head with both hands. It was now very angry. It dropped its hands and ran at Beth Ann.

"Aaaahhh!" she screamed.

Stanley came swinging out from behind the stage curtain. His hands had a firm grasp of the thick curtain rope. Stanley raised his legs up and kicked the surprised gargoyle in the head. The force of the kick sent the gargoyle tumbling into the orchestra pit.

"Whoaa," Stanley said when he swung back behind the curtain and smashed into some boxes. Stanley hit the ground on both feet but fell forward and rolled. The boxes split open when they fell, and costumes poured out. Stanley rolled between the boxes and stopped on a big pile of costumes that the school had used for its production of Romeo and Juliet.

The gargoyle stood up, and its head was stuck in a big brass tuba. Huumpa, huumpa, huumpa was the sound heard when the gargoyle screamed and staggered around, trying to remove the tuba. It stumbled into a set of drums and crashed into the

THE SCHOOL IS BREACHED

cymbals. The gargoyle fell, and the tuba wedged between two large speakers. The gargoyle was lying on its side and could not move. It tried to push its head out of the tuba by grabbing the sides of the tuba and pushing up. While it was doing this, its legs were moving like it was trying to run. After a spurt of energy and effort the gargoyle's body slumped in exhaustion. A very low and slow Hummmmm came from the tuba.

Beth Ann ran to help Stanley. She helped him up from the boxes and costumes. When he was on his feet, she stared into his eyes.

"That was fantastic," she said.

Before Stanley could reply she kissed him on the cheek and he blushed.

SOMETHING COOKING IN THE LAB

Rodney and Sammy ran into the science lab and frantically searched for a place to hide.

"What do we do?" Sammy asked while Rodney looked around for anything to use as a weapon.

"There isn't much here," Rodney said.

They heard a noise and looked to the door. They saw the shadowy head of a gargoyle trying to look through the white-frosted glass that was on the top half of the science lab door. Rodney and Sammy were standing next to two science lab full-length plastic skeletons. They were still wearing their Day of the Dead costumes.

"Stand still," Rodney whispered. "Maybe this thing won't know the difference."

"Are you crazy?" Sammy said.

"We don't know how smart these things are. Maybe it will think we're decomposing cadavers as opposed to our friends who are completely gone," Rodney said, pointing to the skeletons.

They stood perfectly still when the door opened and the gargoyle hopped in. This gargoyle was mean-looking with a thin sharp face and a long pointy chin. Its black beady eyes were deeply set, and there were scars on both cheeks. It was missing the tip of its sharp nose. The stone tip must have been chipped off before it came to life. The gargoyle searched the room. It sniffed the air and hopped over to a trash can. It picked up a half-eaten ham sandwich that had been discarded and gobbled it down. "Ummm," it said, rubbing its belly. Rodney and Sammy made disgusted faces. It then drank the remains of a can of soda that was on a desk. "Brrrrpppp," it let out a long burp.

The gargoyle heard a low squeaking noise and walked over to the hamster cages. It looked in a cage and sniffed the air. It tapped the cage, and a cute light brown-and-white hamster stopped running on its wheel and looked up. It wrinkled and twitched its nose. "Aaaahh," the gargoyle said with a smile and cupped its hands in front of its chest.

The gargoyle gradually made its way to the skeletons. It smelled one of the skeletons and lifted its arm. Sammy was next to this skeleton and stood still. The gargoyle shuffled over to Sammy and smelled his chest. It lifted his arm. Rodney slowly reached back and grabbed an eraser from the blackboard ledge. He threw it at the gargoyle.

"Run!" Rodney yelled.

The eraser slammed into the gargoyle's head, and the white chalk dust flew all over its face and body. It immediately chased Rodney, who threw beakers and test tubes at it. The gargoyle covered its head and body with its wing. The glass bounced off its wing and smashed to the ground. The blows hurt the gargoyle but did not stop it. It gingerly took a few painful steps over the broken glass and then flapped its wings. It flew across the room and grabbed Rodney.

"Help!" Rodney screamed.

The gargoyle smiled an evil smile. It then stopped, put its head up, and sniffed the air.

"Eeeeowwww!" the gargoyle screamed. It let Rodney go and hopped away.

Sammy had lit and held a Bunsen burner under its behind, and it was now burning. It ran out of the science lab, screaming. It ran down the hallway, whimpering in pain and rubbing its rear with both hands.

"Thanks, man. That was quick thinking," Rodney said.

"Who said science lab was a waste of time?" Sammy asked with a smile.

"Let's get back to the gym," Rodney said, and they ran out of the science lab.

LUNCH IS SERVED

Sally ran into the cafeteria. More gargoyles followed her because she was their main focus. They had been offered a precious prize for her capture. The Goblin King promised them continued life in his world, and the gargoyles desired life. They did not want to return to being inanimate stone objects. With this great incentive they spread out to search for Sally.

Sally quickly observed her surroundings and prepared for battle. She:

- Ran to the kitchen's walk-in freezer and gathered items of offensive and defensive value.
- Carried out hard bricks of frozen vegetables, bags of tater tots, and ice cubes.
- Placed her scavenged items behind a long row of cabinets

filled with provisions. There was a stainless steel work surface for preparing food on top of the cabinets.
- Opened the door of a large refrigerator and looked for more ammo.
- Lifted the metal lid of a big pot of tomato soup that was sitting on a shelf, grabbed both handles of the heavy pot, and hauled it to the stove.
- Turned the control and the gas burner lit under the pot.
- Heard the banging, crashing, and skidding of chairs being scattered about the dining room.
- Picked up a kitchen timer and ran back into the freezer.
- Twisted the dial—the timer started to tick—and placed it on a shelf behind some large round containers of vanilla and chocolate ice cream.
- Ran out of the freezer, leaving the door open, and hid behind the cabinets.
- Peered over the cabinets at the door and waited for the gargoyles to enter.
- Put her hand on her chest and breathed deeply to calm down.

The first gargoyle hopped into the kitchen and stared at the open freezer door. This greenish gargoyle had no ears. There was only a small ear hole on each side of its head. It had a large nose, round face, long tail, and deep blue eyes. The funny looking gargoyle also had oversized hands and was a little pudgy around its middle. No Ears walked to the opened freezer door and heard the ticking. It entered and moved the tubs of ice cream out of the way. No Ears picked up the timer, smelled it, and examined it. Sally slammed the freezer door and locked the bolt. The gargoyle looked out of the small window on the top portion of the door. No Ears made a sad facial expression and started to shiver. The unhappy gargoyle began to kick and pound the door with its large fists.

Sally diligently went about her business. She opened the bags of ice cubes and dumped them on the floor in front of the kitchen door. Three gargoyles heard the pounding and converged at the kitchen door. Except for differing heights, they looked identical to the gargoyle trapped in the freezer, like a litter from the same gargoyle mother and father. They looked at each other, and then the three members of the Pudgy No Ear Clan rushed through the kitchen door. They immediately began to slip and slide on the partially melted ice cubes. At first they tried to grab each other for support, but they were all sliding. They eventually lost the struggle to stay upright, and one by one they fell to the floor.

Sally took advantage of their momentary helpless condition and grabbed the now-boiling pot of tomato soup with some oven mitts, waddled to the correct position, put the pot on the floor, and tipped it over. The steaming red liquid contents rushed to greet the fallen gargoyles.

"Eeeeowww!" they howled.

The gargoyles struggled to stand but could not get their footing on the slippery floor. They would get close to standing but would fall again. Sally was doing everything she could to keep them down and out. She hit them with bricks of frozen spinach and handfuls of hard tater tots. She followed this pelting with cans of peas and corn. The gargoyles tried to avoid the edible projectiles, but Sally scored damaging and painful hits to their heads and bodies. The gargoyles whooped, hollered, and screamed when hit with the heavy objects. The gargoyle in the freezer was shivering and watching the horror that had befallen its clan. It winced with each strike and empathized with their pain.

THE SCHOOL IS BREACHED

Sally lined up bags of flour and sugar on the table. Using both hands, she held each bag over her head and lobbed them forward like a human catapult. One by one she sent the bags flying. The five-pound bags hit the gargoyles like exploding bombs. The bags of sugar and flour burst over their bodies and plumed into the air. The sticky mixture of flour, sugar, water, and tomato soup covered the gargoyles' bodies. For dessert Sally served up some pumpkin and coconut custard pies. They hit the gargoyles with a splat and skidded over their bodies. They had lost this food fight and lay writhing in pain.

Sally was out of ammunition. The tough gargoyles were battered, but they slowly began to stand. They limped toward her, holding damaged legs and arms. The three gargoyles surrounded Sally and trapped her in a corner. The shivering gargoyle smiled weakly and clapped its hands together. Sally stood with her fists up, prepared to fight to the end.

Baron Von Muncher bounded into the kitchen and chomped down on the tail of the closest gargoyle and whipped it back and forth. The other gargoyles watched in horror as their kin was jerked violently around. It screamed until the Baron opened his mouth and threw the gargoyle against the wall. Horace bopped it in the head with a meat-tenderizing mallet and then shoved it down a trash chute. The shivering gargoyle watched with a glum look. Baron Von Muncher barked and snapped and herded the gargoyles together. They were the ones now trapped. He gave each the same rough treatment as the first. Horace finished them off and dumped them down the chute. The chute ran to the basement, and they had all piled on top of each other among the garbage in the big green metal container.

Horace smiled at Sally. "I will not refuse to take out the refuse," he said.

Sally laughed but then remembered that the job was not complete. She ran over and opened the freezer door. The gargoyle was covered with frost and shivering. Horace opened the garbage chute and pointed in. Without complaint the rigid gargoyle shuffled over like a penguin and stood at the chute. Horace lifted its stiff body and sent it head first on its dark journey.

Sally ran over and hugged Horace. Baron Von Muncher barked, and Sally turned to greet him. Sally scratched his neck and rubbed his body, and Von Muncher was happy.

"Thank you, boy," she said.

* * *

The Goblin King stood in the middle of the factory floor with a puzzled look and his hand on his chin. The beaten, broken, bruised, burned, swollen, frozen, garbage-smelling, floured, sugared, and milky red-colored gargoyles glumly sat on the floor around him in a circle. Miss Mephisto was at his feet. He looked over the factory. It was operating at full capacity. Enslaved workers were lifting and pushing, machines were pouring and molding, and the candy was spitting out at the end of the assembly line.

"This is harder than I thought," he said. "I need a better plan."

CHAPTER 12

THE SIEGE OF THE GYMNASIUM

Everyone in the gym gathered around Horace. He stood while they sat in the middle of the basketball court. Rodney and Sammy had washed the makeup off their faces.

"We are in the safest part of the school," Horace said. "It is the most defensible, but we have to have a plan of retreat if necessary. If I were the Goblin King, I would attack soon and with overwhelming force. Go now and search the area. Bring anything you think would be useful for our defense."

Everyone stood up and fanned out around the gym to search the offices, closets, and locker rooms.

"If you see a bad guy about, scream and cry out," Horace yelled to them.

The children bedded down to sleep on the floor of the basketball court. They were tired after their stressful day and the repetitious practicing of Horace's defensive plans. Items had been scavenged from the school to make them as comfortable as possible. Towels from the locker room were laid on the gym floor and rolled up into pillows. Blankets and sweat suits used by the sports teams and cheerleaders were now used for bedding and to keep warm.

The lights in the gym were turned off except for a few. The children were trying to sleep, and Horace patrolled the area with Baron Von Muncher at his side. Seth and Jackie sat with their backs leaning against the steel doors at the entrance to the gym. They were charged with guard duty. Seth had his eyes closed, and Jackie was snoring.

It was now late at night. Miss Mephisto walked through the air duct system and came to the vent above the back row of the gym's bleachers. She peeked through the metal strips. Horace was sitting in front of the children. Baron Von Muncher was lying next to Horace, and his eyes were closed. She carefully raised her right paw and wrapped her claws around one of the metal vent bars, grasped it tightly, and pushed it out. She held on after it was removed, twisted it sideways, and pulled it back into the ventilation shaft. It made a small noise when she put it down, and Baron Von Muncher's ears perked up. She waited until the Baron was no longer on alert and softly jumped onto the top row of the bleachers. She carefully made her way down the steps, slinked along the walls of the gym, and stopped at the doors. She crouched down in the shadows when the Baron put his head up and sniffed the air. The Baron then settled back down and closed his eyes.

Miss Mephisto stood up on her hind legs and began to grow. Her body took on a human-like form. She was five feet tall and stood on two legs with feet. She had two arms and two hands with long sharp claws, but she was still covered in black fur and had whiskers and a tail. She quietly walked between Seth and Jackie and stood at the gym doors. Jackie was still snoring, but Seth opened one eye. He looked at Miss Mephisto but did nothing, as if paralyzed with fear. She unbolted the gym doors and then gently tapped on one door. Despite Jackie's snoring the Baron heard this noise. He raised his head, growled, and looked toward the doors. The doors flew open, and Jackie and Seth fell backward. When his back hit the floor, Jackie opened his eyes. Gargoyles were flying over his body and into the gym.

"Red Alert! Red Alert!" he screamed.

The gargoyles flew into the room in a well-executed sneak attack. Jackie's warning activated the first line of defense. The children popped up from their makeshift beds and began executing their well-practiced plans. They did not need much light to complete their tasks. The children quickly raised the volleyball net, and the first wave of gargoyles hit it. Their wings became entangled in the netting. The net filled with gargoyles and crashed to the ground. A second net rose behind it, and more gargoyles were trapped.

Jackie jumped up and turned on the lights. More gargoyles flew in, and the children hit them with dodge balls, knocking them to the ground. A resourceful gargoyle dodged a few balls and then caught one. It laughed but was then hit hard in the side of the head and fell to the ground. More gargoyles flew in, anticipated the thrown balls, and escaped. Some were carrying flaming winged jack-o'-lanterns. They threw them at the children. The evil pumpkins glided in, and the children scattered. The pumpkins hit the gym floor and blew up into fireballs.

"Fall back," Horace yelled.

The children retreated from this firestorm.

Horace, Sally, and her friends picked up some baseball bats. They each had a bucket of baseballs. They each lobbed a ball into the air, swung their bats, and hit the balls at the gargoyles. The baseballs hit their targets and knocked the gargoyles from the sky. One gargoyle smashed on the gym floor behind Sally. It stood up, shook its head, and then began to sneak up on Sally, who was lobbing baseballs and smashing screaming drives at attacking gargoyles. Rodney threw a football in a perfect spiral before a gargoyle could grab her. It hit the gargoyle in the head and knocked it senseless. She turned when it collapsed to the ground and slinked away.

"Thanks," Sally said.

"My pleasure," Rodney said.

The gargoyles kept coming. The Goblin King had added more troops. Horace was knocking them down with his baseball bat, and the Baron was running, jumping, biting, and throwing his victims. Beth Ann was lashing them away with a jump rope. She swung the rope over her head in a circle and hit them with the wooden handle when they came close. Sally was swinging her bat. Stanley, Jackie, Sammy, and Rodney began firing street hockey pucks at them. They stood in a row, held their hockey sticks high, and swung down hard to launch the punishing slap shots. Despite their success, the siege was relentless, and Horace assessed the situation.

"Move toward the back door!" he yelled.

New gargoyles flew in. They were carrying little brown creatures in their outstretched hands. The creatures were about two feet tall and looked like a giant serving of soft chocolate custard from a machine. They were a scary version of the creamy end of an ice cream cone. They had black beady eyes, small mouths, and sharp teeth. They also had stick-thin tiny legs and arms but large hands with exceptionally long, thin index fingers. Their limbs were a lighter shade of brown than their bodies except for the palms of their hands. They were blood red. Horace and the children saw this new threat, and Horace shouted out a warning.

"They're Earbees," he said. "Don't let them near your ears. They can take control of your body."

The gargoyles dropped three Earbees from the sky. They were trying to land them on the backs of the children. Sally and Beth Ann saw them coming and stepped out of the way. The Earbees landed on the ground. They scampered to a dark corner of the gym to wait for another opportunity. The third Earbee landed on Jackie Chambers's back as he was fighting off some gargoyles with his hockey stick. The creature wrapped its legs around Jackie's neck and stuck its index fingers into each one of his ears. Jackie's eyes rolled up into his head. He stopped and dropped his hockey stick. Stanley was next to him swinging his hockey stick wildly. He noticed that Jackie had stopped fighting.

"What's the matter, Jackie?" he said and then noticed the thing on his back.

Jackie turned to him, and Stanley saw the ugly little monster's face. The creature had a little mouth with sharp teeth. Its mouth was opening and closing, and greenish drool was flowing out. Its beady eyes had glazed over in its excitement over having taken control of a victim.

"Aaaahhh!" Stanley screamed. He was too scared to wipe his runny nose.

The creature turned Jackie's head and steered him toward Stanley. Jackie lumbered forward with a stiff-legged gait and reached out to grab at Stanley. The nasty creature's body started to tremble and shake in excitement when it almost had Stanley in its new hands. It laughed in a strange high-pitched tone.

"Geeee-kaha! Geeee-kaha!"

It was so focused on getting Stanley that it did not see the basketball coming toward it at a high velocity. Sammy had made a perfect side-armed throw. The basketball slammed into the creature's soft body. The force of the strike ripped it off of Jackie's head. The upward momentum of the ball carried the creature about fifteen feet before it crashed into the backboard. The creature's soft body flattened out and stuck to the backboard for a moment, and the basketball popped out of the indentation it had made in its body. It fell to the ground and bounced on the basketball court. The creature slowly slid down the backboard and into the hoop. It was caught up in the net and slowly swung back and forth.

"Three points," Sammy yelled and pumped his fist a few times.

"What happened?" Jackie asked, coming out of his trance. "My ears hurt."

Horace was fighting three gargoyles off with his baseball bat. Miss Mephisto in human-like form was sneaking up behind him with her hairy hands up and her sharp claws out.

"Look out, Horace!" Sally yelled.

Horace wheeled around and dodged her slashing claws, which passed within inches of his face. Baron Von Muncher attacked Miss Mephisto. She held him at bay by swinging her claws and hissing while the Baron barked, growled, and snapped. She began to back up because the Baron was relentless in his attack.

Horace held off the gargoyles by swinging his bat with his right hand. With his left hand he reached into a small green pouch tied to his belt at his left side. He removed his hand and sprinkled gold dust onto the Baron. When the dust fell onto the Baron, it glowed bright yellow. Baron Von Muncher began to transform. He slowly turned into a very large human-like Rottweiler with powerful legs, arms, clawed hands, and a large head. He was down on all fours and then stood up like a human. He was over six feet tall, furry, and angry. Miss Mephisto's eyes widened; she hissed, bared her teeth, and ran away.

Baron Von Muncher joined Horace and began fighting in a new way. He jumped high into the air with powerful vertical leaps, snatched the gargoyles from the air with his strong hands, and threw them to the ground. They crashed to the ground and slid to the side of the gym. The bodies piled up quickly. In human-like form Von Muncher was a quick, powerful, fearsome warrior.

Despite their bravery and fighting prowess, the children were forced to retreat toward the back door escape route. The enemy greatly outnumbered them, and they kept on coming with new flying flaming pumpkins, Earbees, and fresh fighting gargoyles. Sally continued to be the main focus of the enemy. During the gradual retreat she was eventually cut off from the others and surrounded by Miss Mephisto and a large number of gargoyles. Horace, Baron Von Muncher, and her friends were engaged in battle and did not see her gradual predicament. Sally saw the formation around her and knew she was in trouble.

"Help!" she screamed.

Horace and Von Muncher ran to protect Sally. Horace stopped and held the Baron back when Miss Mephisto opened her hand. She was holding a Hibernating Hopping Heart Beetle and held it out for all to see. Everyone and everything stopped, and there was an eerie quiet in the vast gymnasium.

"You know what this is, don't you?" Miss Mephisto asked Horace.

"Yes," Horace said.

Miss Mephisto turned to Sally with an evil smile. "Sally, surrender," she said.

"Never!" Sally cried out.

Miss Mephisto smiled again and threw the black ugly bug at Sally.

Horace leaped to try to snatch it from the air, but he missed the bug and tumbled to the ground. The bug was heading toward Sally's heart. Horace looked up and screamed. "No!" he cried with fear in his voice. Sally moved to avoid it, but the beetle landed on her left arm, woke up, and immediately began to chew.

"Oww!" Sally screamed. She grabbed the bug and tried to pull it off, but it would not move. It slowly sunk into her arm.

The toy Valakon clipped to Sally's belt loop began to vibrate and grow. The Yorkshire Terrier-like Valakon grew to about eighteen inches long and came to life. It immediately jumped on Sally's arm. It bit, pulled off, and ate the beetle in one gulp. The Valakon then licked Sally's wound and jumped into her arms. Her cut quickly healed, and she felt no pain. The cute little Valakon looked up into Sally's eyes and smiled. It then turned to Miss Mephisto and the stunned and motionless gargoyles. The Valakon bared its teeth and growled. Its brown eyes turned red. It leapt from Sally's arms, unfurled its flying squirrel-like wings, and flew at the closest gargoyle. It bit the gargoyle in the neck and held on.

"Eeeecckk!" the gargoyle screeched. In an instant the gargoyle turned back into stone and crumbled to the ground.

Miss Mephisto looked at the pile of stones and ran away. The Earbees followed and made high-pitched fearful screams as they scampered away. The gargoyles looked at each other and then took flight. The Valakon flew after them. It bit necks in quick succession, and rocks rained onto the gym floor as gargoyles were destroyed. The rest of them retreated and flew out of the gym. The Valakon chased them all out, turned at the door, and flew back into Sally's arms. It snuggled in her arms. It looked up at her, and its eyes changed from red to blue and then to brown. It made a soft cooing noise and closed its eyes for a nap.

"How?" Sally asked.

"I told you that the Valakon would bring you luck when you needed it most," Horace said and bowed. "I now bow to the magical Valakon and will be its most humble host."

Everyone cheered and hugged. Baron Von Muncher walked to Sally and bowed his head. He then raised it and put his powerful hand on Sally's shoulder and smiled.

"Hello, Sally," he said with a deep voice. "You don't know how happy I am to be able to speak to you like this. It's a miracle."

"I feel the same way, Baron," she said with a smile. "But I must tell you one thing."

"What?" the Baron asked.

"You're naked," she said with a giggle.

"Oh," he said with an embarrassed smile and covered himself. "This is all new to me. I think I'll go over to the maintenance worker's locker room and see if I can find some clothes." He walked away, and Sally laughed to herself.

Horace went to the front doors of the gym to lock them for the night. Before he reached them Hector walked in with Sister Mary and a large group of young children from Saint Bartholomew's Orphanage.

"Did we miss anything?" he asked Horace with a big smile.

"Not at all. Welcome one and all—the tall and the small," Horace replied with a smile and outstretched arms.

He hugged Hector, greeted everyone, and led them into the gym.

CHAPTER 13

THE ROCK LORD

The young children were fed and sleeping on blankets on the gymnasium floor. Sister Mary and Sally's friends were watching the children and guarding the doors. Horace, Hector, Sally, and the Baron sat in a circle to ponder their next move. Horace was quietly speaking to Hector. Sally turned to the Baron to make some small talk before the meeting began. The Baron was wearing a pair of blue denim overalls. He was not wearing a shirt or shoes.

"What was it like being a dog?" Sally asked.

"I am a dog," the Baron replied.

"I mean before you took your current form," Sally said.

"I eat. I sleep. I chase things. I bite things. I bury things. I have few worries. My humans love me, and I love them. It's a good life," he said.

"Did you ever want more?" she asked.

"I really never thought about it," he said and paused. "But, no, I never did. Things could have been worse for me."

Horace stopped speaking to Hector and addressed everyone.

"The situation is very serious," Horace said.

"What can we do?" Sally asked.

"When outnumbered, sometimes the best strategy is a surprise offensive with a small team," Horace replied.

"A direct forceful attack is always my strategy," the Baron said. "Bite them quick and bite them often."

"But it must be a surprise," Hector said.

"Yes, of course, a surprise—and then bite them quick and bite them often," the Baron said and then chomped his teeth.

"I believe we have to attack the Goblin King where he is, and it has to be done immediately," Horace said.

"Isn't that dangerous?" Sally asked.

"Yes, but it is more dangerous to stay here and wait for another attack," Horace said.

"And our defensive strategies have been revealed," Hector said.

"But we can still bite them," the Baron said.

"Yes, my big friend, but they will be many, and we just a few," Hector said.

"We will leave tomorrow to disrupt the Goblin King's plans, but first thing in the morning we must visit with an old friend," Horace said to Sally.

"Who?" Sally asked.

"I will show you tomorrow," Horace replied and put his hand on Sally's shoulder. "But first we must rest so we can do our best," he said with a smile.

They all stood up and checked the children. They then secured the area and lay down to sleep. The Valakon slept next to Sally. Sally felt secure with her friend at her side and quickly fell into a deep sleep.

The next morning Sally, her Valakon, and Horace rose early. They walked together toward Sally's house just as the red sun began to rise. It was visible through the black haze.

"Do you need something from my house before we see your friend?" Sally asked.

Horace stopped in front of Sally's house.

"Our friend is near," Horace replied. He turned toward the Saint Bartholomew rocks that were high on the hill in front of Sally's house. "He is here," Horace said.

"Where?" Sally asked. "I don't see anybody."

"There," Horace said, pointing to the rocks.

They walked to the top of the hill and stopped in front of the rock formation.

"Oh, Rock Lord," Horace said in a loud voice. "It is your old friend Horace."

Horace reached out and touched the rocks. The ground started to rumble and shake. Sally widened her stance and put her arms out to keep her balance. The rocks shifted their position and formed the outline of a face near the peak of the formation.

"Horace, my old friend," the rock formation said in a loud, deep, booming male voice. When the Rock Lord spoke, the rocks that formed the outline of his mouth moved. "Ha, ha ha," he laughed, and the ground rumbled and shook. "The things I have seen you do have brought me great joy."

"Sally Connors is with me," Horace said.

"Ahh, Sally," the Rock Lord said. "I know you well. You visit me often. I was glad you recovered from your accident."

"Thank you, Rock Lord," Sally said with a curtsy.

"I know it was painful for you, but I knew that all would be well," he said.

"And it was," Sally said, smiling at Horace.

"You know why I am here," Horace said.

"Ahh, yes," the Rock Lord said. "It is a sad time. The Goblin King has taken control of the old candy factory, and it is the source of his power and control."

"Should we attack immediately?" Horace asked.

"Yes. You must stop him now. He is ruining the land and water with his waste and destroying the air with his foul, evil smoke. In time he will only grow stronger and take over the

THE ROCK LORD

entire planet. This world will look like his world. You must stop that from happening," the Rock Lord said and finished with a sigh.

"Thank you for your wisdom and counsel," Horace said. "I know what must be done."

"I wish you luck in your challenge," the Rock Lord said. "I will help you when I can. Hopefully, I will have some influence over the outcome."

Horace and Sally thanked the Rock Lord, the ground rumbled, the rocks returned to their old places, and there was silence.

"Come with great haste," Horace said. "Time we must not waste."

Horace and Sally walked down the hill and back to the school.

CHAPTER 14

THE JOURNEY TO THE CANDY FACTORY BEGINS

Everyone prepared for a two-day journey. Food and water supplies from the cafeteria were placed in backpacks along with blankets for sleeping and any other supplies they thought they could use. Horace and Hector supervised and prepared the group. The team included Baron Von Muncher, Sally and her friends, Seth, and, of course, the Valakon, which was always close to Sally. Sister Mary would remain at the school to care for the children.

When preparations were complete, Horace gathered everyone around for instruction.

"We must travel on foot because the Goblin King will have roadblocks. We must stay together and be careful. The land that you know has been changed by the darkness, the foul clouds of smoke, and the gradual leaking of things from the Goblin King's world into your world through the opening he created. They came here like bugs through an open window. You will encounter strange things. You must listen to Hector and me as we make our way to the candy factory. Once we arrive we will improvise and survive."

Everyone nodded in agreement.

"Then let us head out and be free of doubt," Horace said and waved them forward.

With Horace in the lead they marched to the gym doors. The Valakon, perched on the Baron's shoulder, carefully watched Sally. Sister Mary and the children clapped and cheered. Horace opened the door, peeked out, and led them forward.

Sally and her friends were surprised when they left the school and walked outside. Things were deteriorating rapidly. It was dark and overcast. Black smoke drifted past and blocked the red sun. Strange birds flew in the air over the treetops in the distant forest. Large crows gathered in the trees and screeched when they approached. The birds seemed to be warning them to stay out.

"This is horrible," Stanley said, wiping his nose. Sally and the others nodded in silence.

The streets of Somertown were empty, but lights burned in the homes. People had heeded Hector's warnings and locked themselves inside. A few brave, curious people opened their doors as they passed.

"What's happening?" an old man asked. A little boy stood at his side.

"You must stay inside for at least two more days," Hector said. "You must wait until the air clears. If you need food or supplies, go to the school, but be very careful. We will report back with news."

This seemed to satisfy the old man and others who had peeked out of their doors. They closed their doors and locked them.

The group passed the Somertown Lake, and it was filled with thick brown sludge. Some held their noses because the smell was very bad. It was a strong smell of smoke and sulfur, but there was something else that Sally couldn't quite identify. After a moment she concluded that there was a smell of death coming from that ugly sludge. They passed the lake and entered the forest. Going through the forest was the most direct route to the candy factory. Strange spiky-headed creatures poked their heads up and scurried about.

"Eewwww!" Beth Ann said. "What are those things?"

"Don't worry," Hector said. "They are Spikyblinders. Harmless creatures from the Goblin King's world."

"They're still freaky," Rodney said.

They hiked for hours through the forest and then reached a clearing. Horace held his hand up and everyone stopped. Von Muncher and the Valakon sniffed the air. Horace waved everyone forward, and they walked into a large grassy meadow.

"We can rest here but stay near," Horace said.

Everyone took their backpacks off and placed them on the ground.

"What's that?" asked Stanley, pointing.

Stanley wandered over to a dark brown area in the meadow and walked onto it. The spongy material gave way under his feet; it was slippery. He was calm and curious until the brown material moved. Stanley lost his balance and fell down.

"Eewww!" he cried out, looking at the goo on his hands.

He had walked onto a tangle of giant slimy earthworms that were now moving after being rudely disturbed. Everyone gathered around the perimeter of the brown area. Stanley was lying on top of the worms and covered in wormy slime. He couldn't stand because of the slippery slime and the constant slithering movement of the worms. He tried to stand but kept slipping and bouncing on the soft, spongy worms.

"Wow. I could catch a whale using one of those monsters as bait," Jackie said.

Everyone laughed, but Horace reached out his hand.

"Give me your hand," he said. "It will not be funny if you squeeze between them."

Stanley crawled to Horace and reached out his hand.

Everyone stopped laughing when the ground around the perimeter started to crumble and drop. Stanley sank further into the ground and could not reach Horace's hand. They all backed up when the sinkhole started to expand and Stanley dropped further. Stanley was now at risk of being swallowed up by the earth.

"Help!" Stanley screamed.

"We must work together," Horace yelled. "Form a chain."

Horace was at the tip of the chain. Hector held Horace's wrist with his right hand while Horace did the same to Hector. Rodney and Sammy held onto Hector's left wrist and arm. Jackie Chambers wrapped his arms around Rodney's and Sammy's waists. Sally, Beth Ann, and Seth held wrists and wrapped themselves around Jackie's waist. Beth Ann was in the middle, Sally was on the left, and Seth on the right. Sally was able to grab Jackie's belt with her left hand, and Seth was able to do the same with his right hand. Baron Von Muncher held the rear and wrapped his arms around Sally, Beth Ann, and Seth. Horace was lowered into the pit with his feet against the side wall. Everyone else dug their heels into the ground and leaned back a bit.

Horace reached out and was very close to Stanley.

"Rub that slime off your hand," Horace said calmly.

Stanley wiped his hand on a clean part of his shirt and reached up for Horace. Horace grabbed Stanley's hand, but the sinkhole collapsed further. Horace and Stanley dangled in the air.

"Pull hard," Horace yelled.

Everyone pulled. Jackie leaned backward, and the Baron, with his claws and feet digging into the ground, held on. Hector pulled while Horace and Stanley used their feet to climb the wall of the pit—but the dirt kept giving way. Slow progress was made, and they all backed up a bit. Horace was able to get his legs on solid ground and then joined in with the pulling.

Stanley rose from the pit. He was almost out of the pit when Seth let go and fell to the ground.

"I can't hold on!" Sally screamed.

Everyone in front fell forward when the chain broke, and the Baron fell backward a bit. He still held Seth, whose body was limp and eyes were closed. Everyone in front slid forward while Horace and Stanley fell further into the pit. They grunted and strained but were losing ground.

"Pull!" Jackie desperately yelled.

The Baron dropped Seth to the ground, and his eyes went wild with anger.

"Graaahh!" the Baron let out a great roar and jumped forward. He moved Beth Ann and Sally out of the way and grabbed Jackie around the waist. He dug his clawed feet into the dirt and pulled. He backed up with his powerful legs, pulling the whole chain with him. He growled as he moved. Seth opened his eyes and watched. Horace and Stanley rose out of the pit to safety.

Seth sat on the ground and shook his head. The Baron glared at him with wild eyes and growled.

"It wasn't my fault," Seth said. "I passed out."

Sally put her hand on the Baron's arm to try to calm his animal instincts.

"It's okay," Sally said. "Everyone's fine. Leave it alone."

The Baron calmed down but continued to stare at Seth. Sally and her friends trudged a safe distance from the lip of the sinkhole and collapsed to the ground in exhaustion. Horace, Hector, and Baron Von Muncher remained standing and scouted the area for more danger as the others rested.

"We must continue and cover some more miles before dark," Horace said. "Rest for a while and recover your spark."

Sally and her friends groaned.

"And, Stanley," Horace said, "don't use more than one bottle of water to clean that slime off. We have to preserve. We have to conserve."

Stanley groaned some more, and everyone else chuckled softly.

CHAPTER 15

A Friend and Foe in the Forest

Once they were rested they continued their journey. They entered the forest again and walked in silence. They now recognized and contemplated the danger that existed in their transformed town.

It was getting late as they reached a small clearing.

"We will sleep here, where it is clear," Horace said and put his backpack on the ground.

Everyone plopped their backpacks on the ground and rummaged through them for food. The Baron had nothing in his backpack but bottles of water and dog biscuits. Sally was still wondering why the school cafeteria had so many dog biscuits. Sammy and Rodney had made peanut butter and jelly sandwiches and cheese sandwiches. Beth Ann had a salad in a plastic container with salad dressing and some fruit. Stanley had chocolate cake. Sally had granola bars, fruit, and a baloney sandwich. Seth had a big piece of ham. Jackie had stuffed his backpack with rectangular slices of frozen pizza. They were now thawed, and he ate them raw.

They sat around in a circle and enjoyed their meal. Horace and Hector did not eat.

"What do you have there, big guy?" Stanley asked the Baron.

"Biscuits," he replied. "Beef, chicken, and cheese. They are the perfect traveling food. Want one?" he asked, holding a biscuit out to Stanley.

"No thanks," Stanley said.

"I'll try one," Jackie said.

He grabbed the cheese biscuit that was offered by the Baron and bit off a big piece. It crumbled and crunched in his mouth when he chewed.

"Hey, that's pretty good. Want some pizza?" Jackie asked, offering a piece to the Baron.

The Baron took the piece and smelled it. He chomped the whole piece with one bite, and Jackie smiled.

"I like the way you eat," he said.

"It was tasty," the Baron said. "I'll trade you a meat biscuit for another. Meat is the best."

Jackie agreed to the deal, and the exchange was made. They munched their food, and both parties were very happy with the bargain.

Stanley was merrily gobbling his chocolate cake. Beth Ann stared at him and slowly raised pieces of her salad to her mouth and chewed them slowly.

"Is that all you're going to eat?" she asked Stanley.

"Yes, I love cake," Stanley replied.

"That's not very healthy for you," Beth Ann said.

"Sure it is," Stanley said. "It has your slow energy cake calories and your fast energy icing calories. Besides, this could be my last meal, so I'm not worried about my health."

"Good point," Sally said.

Beth Ann thought for a moment and continued to stare at Stanley's cake.

"I'll trade you an apple for some cake," she said, holding the apple out.

Stanley looked at the apple for a long moment.

"I'm not a huge fan of apples," he said. Beth Ann made a pouting face. "But since I like you, I'll make the trade."

Beth Ann smiled and gave him her apple. Stanley gave her a big piece of chocolate cake. She quickly took a big bite and started to giggle.

"It's better than that salad, isn't it?" Stanley asked.

Beth Ann nodded because her mouth was still filled with the cake.

Sammy and Rodney quietly munched on their sandwiches while Sally took a bite of her granola bar. She offered some to Horace and Hector. Hector took a bar and thanked her, but Horace declined.

"No thanks," Horace said. "I can't eat when I'm worried."

"Do you think we have a good chance?" Sally asked.

"We have a chance," Horace replied. "I'm going to keep watch."

Horace stood up and began to patrol the area.

"He's very serious," Sally said to Hector.

"He's always serious when there is a battle to be won or an important task to be accomplished," Hector said.

"How long have you known him?" Sally asked.

"Since I was very young," Hector replied. "I knew of Horace before I was awarded the honor of being his apprentice. He is very famous in our world."

"Wow," Sally said. "I knew he was special."

"Yes," Hector said. "Wow, he is."

Sally and Hector ate their granola bars and watched Horace patrol the area. Sally gave the Valakon pieces of her bar, which it ate quickly.

After the meal Horace and Hector made a campfire while everyone took out their blankets and tried to get comfortable. After a long, active, and anxious day everyone was exhausted. Sally and her friends were not used to sleeping on the ground.

The Baron did not have this problem and simply curled up on the ground next to Sally. It was a bit chilly, so Sally lay next to his back to stay warm. It was very dark in the woods, but a small amount of light would appear when the full moon was not covered by a black smoke cloud. The quiet would be interrupted by strange shrieks in the forest, and Sally and her friends were nervous. The only one sleeping soundly was the Baron, and he was snoring loudly. Stanley giggled after a particularly loud snore.

"Shusssh," Sally said. "Go to sleep."

Time passed and the forest became quiet. There were no more strange shrieks, and the campfire burned down to a low flame. Everyone was sleeping except for Horace and Hector, who sat together. A rustling sound came from one side of the campsite, and Sally woke up with wide eyes.

"What's that noise?" she whispered

The Baron popped his head up and sniffed in the direction of the sound. He pounced in the dark.

"Squeee, squeee!"

Something was squealing loudly, and people were jumping, screaming in fear, and running around. Sally tried to be calm in the commotion and searched her backpack for her emergency light. She felt the handle and pulled it out. She flipped the switch on and waved the light over the area. She flashed across the frightened faces of her friends. They were all wearing their backpacks. Horace had instructed them to always grab their backpacks in an emergency situation. They had learned well. She found the Baron and kept the light on him. He was standing near his backpack and was holding a strange, small, scared, and squealing animal by the neck with one hand. It looked like a giant hairless rat with pinkish white skin and dark pink eyes.

"What the heck is that thing?" Stanley screamed in a high voice.

"It's a Naked Katawamp," Horace said with a laugh. "Don't worry—it's harmless. It's a very intelligent herbivore, and it's always looking for a meal and more."

Everyone, with the exception of Horace and Hector, was surprised when the animal spoke.

"Leave me. Leave me," it pleaded, looking up at the Baron.

"Holy cow," Stanley said and stated the obvious. "It talks."

"I told you they were very intelligent. Which way is the best route to the candy factory?" Horace asked the animal in a serious tone.

"No involve now!" it said.

"You already are involved, my friend," Horace said.

"Goblin King evil," it said with its head down.

"Which way?" Horace repeated.

"No involve," the Katawamp said, shaking its head. "No—no involve."

Horace turned to the Baron and winked.

"Him you can eat, from head to feet," he said loudly to the Baron.

The Baron lifted the animal, opened his mouth, and bared his large teeth.

"Squeee-no. Squeee-no," the Katawamp said, covering its eyes with its small hands.

"Well?" Horace asked.

The Naked Katawamp pointed its nose in a direction north and moved its head up and down.

"Thank you for your kind help," Horace said. "There is no more need to yelp."

The Baron lowered the Katawamp from his mouth. The animal began to sniff the air maniacally, and its body began to shake.

"Danger, danger!" it squealed and pointed its nose toward the forest.

Sally swung her light in that direction, just as an animal ran out from behind a tree and leapt at Rodney.

"Aahhh!" Rodney screamed.

The animal had a head like a wolf and ferociously bit down on Rodney's backpack. The animal dragged Rodney to the ground and whipped its head back and forth, trying to rip the backpack away. Rodney screamed as he was thrown back and forth by the powerful animal. Sally kept her light on Rodney, and everyone could see that the animal had a body like a muscular miniature pony.

"It's a Feral Devil," Horace yelled. "They're carnivores, and there will be others."

Beth Ann reacted quickly. She emerged from the darkness and bravely kicked the animal in its hind leg with her stylishly pointed Goth vampire boots.

"Eeeep!" the animal cried out.

It released Rodney's backpack and ran away.

"Gather together around Sally," Horace commanded.

They grouped together, and Horace grabbed Sally's emergency light. He held it up and waved it around in a circle. They were surrounded by a pack of snarling Feral Devils, who were grinding their fangs and drooling in anticipation of a meal.

The animals began to growl and moved closer. Rodney pulled a lighter from his backpack and whispered to Sammy. He pulled a roll of toilet paper out of his backpack and held it out to Rodney. Rodney lit the toilet paper, and Sammy threw it at the animals. The flaming toilet paper flew up and then down in a slow arc toward the animals, and they scattered. The toilet paper hit the ground and bounced around. When the fire died out, the animals returned to their positions.

"They are pack animals," Horace said to Baron Von Muncher. "You know what to do."

The Baron nodded and put the Naked Katawamp on the ground. It scurried away and hid under a blanket. The Baron stepped forward and scanned the pack of Feral Devils. He focused on the largest animal in front of the pack. The Baron quickly moved toward it. Horace kept the light on the action.

The Baron and the large animal growled at each other. They circled, and each made a charge and backed off. During the Baron's charge the animal had turned around and kicked out with its powerful legs. The Baron avoided the kick, and they continued to circle.

Another animal moved forward to join the attack. It crept up behind Baron Von Muncher. The Valakon flew at the animal and attacked. The animal ran, and the others in the pack backed off.

The large Feral Devil used this distraction. It leapt at the Baron and tried to bite his throat. The Baron caught the animal under its front legs. The snapping teeth were inches from his neck. He lifted the animal high in the air and threw it at the pack. The Feral Devil landed, tumbled on the ground, and lay silent.

The other animals gathered around. The battered leader slowly moved and then stood up. The Valakon jumped onto Von Muncher's shoulder. The lead animal looked at them, and they both growled. The defeated Feral Devil turned and trotted away. The others followed.

"That was fantastic!" Sally said.

Everyone gathered around the Baron and congratulated him. Horace gave the emergency light back to Sally. They stopped when they heard a rustling noise. Sally quickly turned the light toward the blankets scattered on the ground. The Naked Katawamp poked his head out from under one.

"Danger gone?" the Katawamp asked and everyone laughed. "I stay?"

Horace walked over and picked up the Naked Katawamp and smiled. "You can stay, I say," he said.

The Naked Katawamp breathed a sigh of relief, and everyone laughed again.

They all tried to calm down after this excitement and get some much-needed sleep.

CHAPTER 16

A Difficult Hill to Climb

"Help! Help!"

Everyone woke up at daybreak when a great commotion arose at the campsite. Stanley was screaming, and Horace, Hector, and the Baron were running. The Valakon was flying, and the Naked Katawump was scampering. Sally and her friends were groggy and confused but rose up and followed the running bodies to the spot where they stopped and gathered. They woke up completely when they saw what had happened during the night.

Stanley was in a panic and could not get out from under his blanket. A Bingbat Bug had silently crawled in during the night and coated the entire blanket and Stanley's head with its excretion.

Stanley's face was obscured but visible under the transparent coating. It looked like a sheer white fabric was covering his face. He was scared, breathing hard, and almost hyperventilating. Stanley and his blanket were stuck to the ground. The bug was not around. It had secured Stanley and was saving him for later.

Horace and Hector relaxed a bit after they assessed the situation.

"A Bingbat Bug chose you for its next meal," Hector said to Stanley in a very calm manner, but it did not calm Stanley down at all.

"Get me out!" Stanley screamed in a very high-pitched voice. His visible mouth opened and closed while he spoke, and his face contorted in fear under the coating. "I don't want to be a meal."

Sally looked at her friends, and they all nodded. They all felt that Stanley had made a very reasonable request, one that they all would have made if they found themselves in similar circumstances.

"Use your claws," Horace said to the Baron.

Baron Von Muncher knelt down and used his sharp claws to scrape the excretion where it met the ground. With great difficulty he was able to dig a little under the ground and then pull the coating off of Stanley in one piece.

"This material is very strong," the Baron said as he pulled it off.

Stanley in a manic burst scampered out from under the blanket and collapsed a few feet away. He was still scared and breathing heavily. Sally worried that he was in shock as he lay on the ground in the fetal position. Everyone gathered around to calm him. Sally put her hand on his shoulder, and Beth Ann sat down and held his hand.

"Relax, Stanley," Jackie said. "You ain't been eaten, pardner."

"I almost was!" Stanley screamed.

"Almost don't count," Rodney said.

"Yes. That is correct," the Baron said. "You either have been eaten or you have not been eaten."

"In whole or in part," Sally said to clarify.

"Of course," the Baron said. "You have not been eaten in whole or in part."

"I guess you could have been suffocated," Sammy said.

"That's right," Stanley said. "I could have suffocated."

"Don't be silly," Beth Ann said. "You were breathing fine through that gunk."

Horace and Hector looked at each other and smiled. They were generally amused by the whole conversation.

While Stanley engaged in the conversation he had gradually calmed down and was now breathing regularly. The concept of "almost" versus "fact" took his mind away from the fact that he had almost been eaten and/or suffocated. Beth Ann continued to hold his hand, and she smiled at him. Stanley smiled back.

Things finally settled down, and it was time to eat breakfast. Jackie Chambers reached for his backpack. He poked his hand in, rummaged about, and pulled out a large bag of barbecue potato chips. He ripped the bag open and began to eat. He jammed a big handful into his mouth and started crunching. Crumbs dribbled down his chin and over his clothes.

"That's your breakfast?" Beth Ann asked.

Jackie held his finger up and continued to chew. He swallowed and then took a drink of water.

"Sure," he replied. "It's health food. You got potato, your vegetable group, and your salt and spice group."

He smiled at Stanley, and Stanley smiled and nodded in agreement.

Beth Ann just shook her head in disbelief and munched on her apple. Sally passed around a box of cornflakes and a quart of milk in a plastic bottle. She had packed the milk in an insulated bag so it would not spoil. Everyone took turns pouring the cornflakes into their mouths and following up with a milk chaser. After taking their big gulps, they all had milk mustaches.

"Does anyone miss school?" Sally asked.

"Maybe a little," Stanley said.

"Not me," Jackie said. "I hate school, especially math."

Sammy and Rodney nodded their heads in agreement as they chewed their cereal.

"I wonder if we'll ever have our Halloween dance?" Sally asked.

"Who knows at this point," Stanley replied.

The Naked Katawamp stuck his nose into the cereal box.

"Hey!" Sally yelled and grabbed the box.

"Me hungry too," the Katawamp whined.

"Okay," Sally said and sprinkled some cornflakes on the ground. The Katawamp picked a flake up with its front paws and nibbled on it. "Ummm, ummm," it said and then quickly gobbled it up and excitedly moved on to the next flake. Everyone laughed when they watched the Naked Katawamp joyfully eating. After each flake it would say "Ummm," rub its little belly, and then grab another flake.

"Do you have a name?" Sally asked the Katawamp.

"My friends call me Magpo," it said between bites.

"What does it mean?" Sally asked.

"Magnificently polite," it said, and everyone laughed.

"What funny?" Magpo asked.

"How did you get here?" Sally asked.

"Me not know," Magpo said, shaking his head. "Strange feel. Bright light then me lost. No find fee (family). Bugs me eat. Bad bad. No happy."

Jackie watched the Katawamp. He sniffed the air and then picked up the Katawamp, who continued to hold the cornflake in its little hands and merrily munch away. Jackie sniffed the air again.

"I didn't notice before, but this little guy smells like freshly popped popcorn," Jackie said.

Everyone gathered around to smell, and they all agreed. Magpo was enjoying the attention until Jackie held him to his nose and huffed deeply.

"Aaaahhh," he said. "That's good stuff."

Magpo looked miserable while everyone else laughed.

Beth Ann finished eating and yelled to Horace.

"Where do we go to the bathroom?" She asked.

Horace pointed to the woods.

"Eewww!" Beth Ann shrieked. "No way."

She thought about it for a moment and then stood up. Sammy threw her a roll of toilet paper, and she caught it. She walked toward the woods.

"Don't forget to act like a mole and dig a hole," Horace yelled to her.

"Eewww!" she said without turning around and walked into the woods.

Sally and her friends laughed and then looked at each other. One by one they stood up and followed Beth Ann into the woods.

* * *

They gathered their gear together to continue the trek to the candy factory. Horace doused the remains of the campfire with water, and Hector stirred it with a stick.

They marched forward. Hector took the point position to warn the others if there was danger ahead. After a while he ran back to Horace and whispered in his ear. Horace waved everyone toward him, and they gathered around. He spoke to them quietly.

"There is a herd of Cedebeasts close by," he said. "They are very dangerous animals, and we don't want to rouse them."

They proceeded carefully and quietly in single file. The Baron guarded the rear. He was right behind Seth and watched him carefully. A large meadow appeared to their left when they cleared some trees. Sally and her friends were surprised, wide-eyed, and nervous when they saw a herd of large animals grazing. They were the size of a very large and extraordinarily muscular bull. Their heads were similar to a male lion but much larger with a black mane. They did not have whiskers or fur. The skin on their faces and bodies was black and leathery. Sally could see that their teeth were razor sharp.

Hector was still at the point, and he ducked down. Horace followed his lead and motioned for everyone to do the same. They all walked in a crouch as Hector led them into a shallow gully behind a row of bushes. As the group moved forward, the Cedebeasts would snort and loudly roar at times as they fought for small areas of grazing territory. They bucked their heads up and down and made aggressive charges at members of the herd that wandered too close.

Sally and her friends were scared every time they heard these roars and scuffles. Sally was particularly worried about Stanley. His face was very pale, and he had not completely recovered from his encounter with the Bingbat Bug.

After one very loud roar Beth Ann jumped in fear and then stumbled to the ground. She made some noise, and everyone stopped. Hector held up his hand for everyone to stay very still. Sally looked through the bushes and saw that the entire herd of Cedebeasts had stopped grazing and were looking in their direction. Their noses twitched as they smelled the air. After a few tense moments they began to graze again. Hector put his hand down, and they moved forward.

After a few minutes they cleared the meadow and made it back into the forest and to safety. Horace and Hector felt comfortable enough to stop for a rest. They all were glad to have this quiet time to calm down.

Fear and nervousness had exhausted them, and they collapsed to the ground in relief.

After their short rest they hiked for a while until they reached a high rocky hill. They began to climb the steep hill.

Horace stopped when he heard some movement and grunting sounds. He held his hand up, and everyone stopped. He put his finger to his lips to warn them to be quiet. Horace pointed to some trees that were at the bottom of the hill. Sleeping in a pack were some strange animals. At times the animals would grunt and turn on their sides to get comfortable. The group was downwind from the animals. Sally and her friends made disgusted faces when their malodorous smells wafted past their noses.

The animals were dotted in the front of their bodies like a leopard and striped in the back like a zebra. The dots were black on white skin, and the stripes were black on orange skin. Their skin was like an elephant's, and they had a similar long trunk with a large, wide mouth below it. The animals had spiny backs and were large. Each was about the size of a hippopotamus.

Horace waved everyone forward. They quietly climbed the hill and stepped carefully. They did not want to make any noise that would disturb the sleeping animals. Halfway up the hill Seth stepped on a pile of rocks and dislodged them. Everyone froze and watched the rocks roll down the hill. They were relieved when the rocks rolled to the bottom of the hill but did not wake the animals. One final rock rolled a little farther than the others. They watched it reach the bottom of the hill, roll slowly past the trees, and gently bump one of the animals. It did not open its eyes, but its trunk popped into the air. It sniffed the air and turned like a periscope. It continued to sniff and stopped when it was pointed toward the group on the hill.

"Wallleeee!" it screamed in a loud, high-pitched tone.

They all held their hands over their ears.

"It hurts!" Stanley screamed.

All of the animals woke, jumped up, and charged to the hill.

"Run!" Horace yelled.

Horace held his ground, and the others made a mad scramble to the top of the hill. He then followed. The animals' trunks expanded in diameter and made a sucking noise as they ran up the hill. Their black eyes grew large and wide. The hill began to rumble and shake. Loose rocks began to avalanche down the hill. Sally and her friends ducked out of the way and barely avoided them. The rocks hit the animals and sent them tumbling down the hill. Some animals sucked the large rocks into their trunks, and the force knocked them backward. They rolled down the hill, trying to blow the rocks out. They continued this effort until they smashed into the trees at the bottom of the hill. When they hit the trees, the rocks shot out, and they collapsed to the ground. Others sucked in smaller rocks and stones and were able to shoot them out while they kept charging. Everyone ducked and moved to avoid these dangerous projectiles as they hit the ground like bullets and ricocheted off surrounding rocks.

Horace jumped out of the way of the tumbling rocks and rolled on the ground to avoid more. Sally turned to see that one of the creatures had avoided the rocks and was moving toward Horace. Sally ran down the hill to help him. Horace stood up with his back toward the animal. It raised its trunk to attack.

"Horace!" Sally yelled and pushed him away.

The animal turned its trunk to Sally.

"Run away from its mouth!" Horace yelled. "It's a Spiny Vacusucker."

Sally tried to run, but the animal moved quickly. Its trunk expanded when it started to suck in air. The incoming air created a strong vacuum pull, and the entering air was expelled through a blowhole on its back. The animal's trunk was like a large, powerful vacuum cleaner. Sally heard the sucking sound of the moving air and felt the pulling pressure. She fell and was pulled forward by the strong suction. Her feet went into the animal's mouth. She twisted her torso and wrapped her arms around a rock that was embedded in the hillside. She desperately held on.

The Vacusucker's eyes grew wide, and it sucked harder. It positioned its flexible trunk over Sally. The trunk moved closer, and her body rose to meet it. She felt the pressure on her back when the tip of the trunk began to touch her. The sucking sound became muffled when the trunk firmly attached to her back. The Vacusucker then used its trunk to drag her further into its mouth. Sally's hold began to give way. Horace grabbed Sally's arms and pulled. She stopped moving further into the mouth, but the animal was relentless. It increased the suction, and her legs slowly inched further into the animal's mouth. The Baron ran in and grabbed Sally around the waist. Hector rushed in and held onto Horace.

"Grrr-kiack," the Valakon growled and screeched at the animal.

The Vacusucker's eyes looked up when the Valakon launched into the air, but it did not stop pulling Sally.

The Valakon landed on the animal's back and jammed a stone into its blowhole. The Vacusucker made a funny face and swung its trunk up to swat the Valakon. The Valakon easily avoided this attack. The Vacusucker continued to suck in air and its body began to inflate like a blowfish. The Vacusucker looked like it was about to explode, and it spit Sally out. She fell into Horace's arms. The Spiny Vacusucker then shot away when the air from its body expelled quickly out of its trunk. It was slightly off the ground when it completely deflated like a balloon losing air. It crashed to the ground and rolled down the hill. When it stopped rolling, it stood up and ran away. A muffled uummp, uummp, uummp was heard as it strained to eject the stone from its blowhole. After a few attempts the stone shot high into the air and out of sight.

"Are you injured?" Horace asked Sally.

"I'm fine," Sally said, rubbing her legs.

"Don't put yourself in danger like that," Horace said sternly. "I can take care of myself."

"Everyone needs help at times," Sally snapped. "You're welcome."

Sally ran up the hill to join her friends. Horace looked at Hector and the Baron. Hector held his hands up and shrugged his shoulders. The Baron laughed a deep laugh.

CHAPTER 17

THE RIVER CROSSING

Everyone gathered at the top of the hill. They looked over the valley; the Somertown Candy Factory was visible in the distance. It was situated along the winding river that fed the Somertown Lake. Black smoke was billowing out of three large chimneys, gathering above, and moving with the wind. At times the wind would swirl, and the smoke scattered in all directions.

"That's our destination," Horace said. "Our journey is almost over."

"There," Hector said, pointing to a part of the river that narrowed.

"I agree," Horace said. "We will cross there."

"Cross the river," Beth Ann groaned. "I didn't bring my swimsuit."

The boys chuckled, but Sally was serious. "We might as well get started," she said.

Everyone agreed, and they started to make their way down the hill.

They hiked through the forest with Hector in the lead. They emerged at the river's bank at the precise spot Hector had pointed out. Everyone removed their backpacks and sat down to rest under some trees. Jackie immediately pulled out a bag of potato chips and began eating while the others drank some water. Hector walked to the bank and began to search along the ground. He picked up a stick and then discarded it. Stanley joined him.

A tiny animal jumped out of the murky river and onto land. It looked like a smaller-than-usual Chihuahua with a coat of short black hair and bright incandescent green eyes. It also had a set of gills like a fish. They were clearly visible under each ear. It stood up on its back legs and sniffed the air. It got down on all fours and started to walk toward Jackie. Additional animals jumped up behind it, and a pack of nine walked toward Jackie in single file.

"Aaaahhh!" Beth Ann screamed and jumped to her feet, pointing. "What are those things?"

Rodney and Sammy also rose, but Jackie, Horace, and the Baron remained calm. Magpo was curled in a ball and raised his head. "Phaa-la," he said in disdain while lowering his head and closing his eyes. These creatures were of no concern to him. Jackie continued to contentedly eat his chips. The animals crawled all over his lap and snapped up the crumbs.

"Cha-heek. Cheek-cheek-cheek," the leader happily chirped in a high-pitched tone, and then the others joined in excitedly. The leader stopped, and all was quiet for a moment. It chirped again, and the others followed. They were a very rowdy and animated little group. One of them crawled up on his shoulder and watched him eat. Jackie didn't seem to mind at all. He just focused on his chips.

Beth Ann was stunned. "Are you going to let them crawl all over you?"

"They seem harmless," Jackie said casually. "They just want some food. I can understand that."

Beth Ann stared at Horace and the Baron with her mouth wide open. They both chuckled.

"They're Aquacanes," Horace said. "They are completely harmless and a good-luck sign. They used to live only on land but adapted to the water over time. They will eat until their little bellies bloat and can do nothing but float."

Beth Ann and her friends calmed down, and Jackie fed a piece of chip to the Aquacane on his shoulder.

Stanley watched Hector for a while but couldn't figure out what he was doing. Hector continued to look down and search along the ground.

"What are you doing?" Stanley finally asked.

"I need a long stick to check the depth of this river," he replied.

Stanley helped him search and found a pile of nice long straight thick sticks.

"How about this one?" he asked, holding it up.

"That's perfect," Hector said.

Hector climbed down the bank and put the long stick into the water that had been thickened and darkened by the sludge that poured out of the candy factory. He pushed it down all the way, and it did not touch bottom.

"It's deeper than I hoped," he said to Stanley.

He lifted the stick, which was now covered with brown, sticky, slimy sludge.

"That's disgusting," Stanley said. "Do we have to swim through that junk?"

"It's also thicker than I thought it would be," Hector said. "And yes, we will have to swim through it."

All of the Aquacanes stopped and stared at the river. The one on Jackie's shoulder jumped down and ran. They all chirped, scampered to the river, and jumped into the water.

"Hey, something really spooked those little guys," Jackie said.

Horace stood up with a concerned look and scanned the area.

Hector walked along and continued to probe the water with his stick. He pulled it up at times and showed the sludge line to

Stanley. Without warning the head of a giant black serpent shot out of the thick murky water and chomped down on Hector's stick with its sharp fangs. Stanley screamed, backed up quickly, stumbled, fell to the ground, and passed out. Everyone started screaming when they saw the creature. It spit Hector's stick out of its mouth and swiveled its head from side to side. Its black eyes stared at each potential victim as its head slowly moved. The serpent's tongue darted out and in.

Horace and the Baron ran to protect Hector. Sally and Beth Ann dragged Stanley to safety. Sammy, Rodney, Jackie, and Seth gathered large, long sticks for protection. They passed them out to everyone. The Baron quickly snapped, chewed, and clawed off any protrusions so the staffs were in proper fighting form for everyone.

The serpent dove under water, and then its head rose up from the center of the river. Another head rose up about five feet from the first. The heads were identical. Both serpents rose with their snakelike body about ten feet out of the water. They stared at everyone and opened their mouths at the same time. They hissed with their fangs showing and their long serpent tongues flicking in the air.

"Do you think there are more than two?" Sally asked Horace.

"No," Horace replied. "There is only one. It is a Narcisserpent. They have identical heads at each end of its body."

The two heads moved closer together. The two ends of the creature's body intertwined until the heads were very close to each other. The two heads stared at each other and flicked their tongues out until they touched. Then they unraveled and disappeared under the water.

"This is bad," Horace said. "We must defeat this serpent to move on."

The two heads burst out of the water and began snapping at everyone on the bank. They hit the heads with their sticks, and the creature disappeared under the water. After a moment it attacked again. It used its heads to splash water at them. The water hit Beth Ann, and it slimed over her arm. "Eeeewww!" she said, making a disgusted face and wiping it off. The heads looked at each other. Both heads nodded; they seemed to be snickering and laughing.

Recognizing that they were pinned down, the Baron aggressively moved to the bank of the river. The serpent focused on him, and he ducked and weaved as the heads tried to inflict deadly bites. The Baron carefully watched and studied the movement of the heads. He then made a bold move. His hands quickly shot out and grabbed the neck of each head. The heads furiously whipped around. The Baron held on until the heads moved powerfully in different directions. The head in his right hand moved down and toward the Baron's left foot while the head in his left hand shot quickly over the Baron's head. This movement flipped the Baron off his feet. He released the necks and tumbled to the ground. He rolled and ended up lying face down. The serpent attacked while the Baron was vulnerable, but Sally and her friends hit the heads with their staffs. This gave the Baron time to recover and get back to his feet.

The Baron was neither afraid of the Narcisserpent's strength nor embarrassed for being thrown. He was just angrier and more persistent. He stood with wild eyes and looked around. Always planning, he stared at a rock formation that rose high above the river. He ran to it and climbed up. He stood on a ledge and growled. This attracted the Narcisserpent's attention. It seemed especially interested in sinking its fangs into the Baron. It positioned itself between the Baron and the others.

The head closest to the Baron watched him while the other head watched the others. The Baron pointed at the Valakon and got its attention. He then pointed at the serpent's head that was closest to the Valakon. With no further communication the

Valakon launched into the air and attacked that head. When the head closest to the Baron turned to watch this attack, the Baron leaped onto the serpent's body. He put his right arm around the serpent's neck just under its head and squeezed.

"Aaaagggg-hisss," the serpent hissed as it tried to whip the Baron off of its neck. The Baron held on and squeezed tighter. The serpent violently whipped its neck back and forth, but the Baron did not budge. The other head stopped snapping at the Valakon and plunged under the water. It emerged to attack the Baron. The Baron swatted the second head with his left hand and his sharp claws tore into the serpent's face and drew blood. Both heads shrieked in pain. The Valakon resumed its attack, and the Baron sunk his large canines into the serpent's neck. Blood gushed, and both heads shrieked. The second head backed away from the Baron and the Valakon. Both heads swayed back and forth in pain and confusion. After a moment of staring at each other, both heads plunged under water and disappeared with the Baron.

"Baron!" Sally screamed.

Everyone ran to the bank and scanned the surface of the water.

"There!" Beth Ann yelled, pointing to the right.

The trailing head without the Baron popped out of the water as the serpent swam away. It hissed at everyone as it moved away and then slowly pulled its head back under water.

Sally began to cry. Horace and Hector comforted her while the others continued to scan the water in the hope that the Baron would emerge.

"He was a good friend," Horace said. "He bravely gave his life for our cause. I will miss him greatly."

Sally cried on Horace's shoulder, and a tear ran down Horace's cheek.

"What happened?" Stanley asked, waking up.

Magpo popped his head out of a backpack.

"We still have to find a way to cross that river," Horace said.

He knew that in battle you cannot afford to think about the loss of a friend for too long. He gathered everyone around for a moment of silence.

The ground and the rock formation began to rumble and shake. The river began to bubble, and a rock bridge rose from the water and fully spanned the river.

"It is always good to be friends with the Rock Lord," Horace said. "Gather your things and let's move forward."

They quietly gathered their things. They were devastated and in shock. Everyone was suffering a great sadness for the loss of a great friend. They moved slowly with anguished looks, but all agreed that the Baron would have wanted them to march forward aggressively. They also all agreed that they would avenge his death by completing their mission. They put their backpacks on and prepared to cross the river. They used their strong sticks as staffs to help them hike the final miles.

CHAPTER 18

A
Revelation

The Goblin King looked out of his office window and watched his candy being produced. He rubbed his chin with his hand. Miss Mephisto was curled up in a comfy chair. A gargoyle with scars on his face stood in front of the Goblin King's desk.

"What's that sneaky elf up to?" he asked and then turned to the gargoyle. "Anything happening at the school?"

The gargoyle shook his head no.

"Hummmm, he must be hiding in fear," the Goblin King said. "Are your gargoyles healthy yet?"

The gargoyle nodded his head yes.

"Start preparing for another attack," he said. "Get out of here. There will be no excuses this time."

He turned back to the window as the gargoyle scampered out of the office. He watched the gargoyle hop down the steps and then looked up to watch a forklift carry a large load of candy into the warehouse to be loaded into a delivery van.

"Finally the end," he said with an evil chuckle.

The dark brown candy van was loaded, and the driver and his assistant got in and drove off. They drove out of the warehouse and out to the road on their mission to infect more people with the evil candy. Even in their red-eyed zombie-like state they were still surprised when they looked down the road. They stared at each other in confusion.

Sally and Beth Ann were standing in the middle of the road, waving.

"Hello!" Sally yelled.

The van pulled up and rolled to a stop.

"You-hooo," Beth Ann said. "Can you help us, you cute red-eyed guys?"

The driver and his assistant got out of the van and began acting according to their preprogrammed agenda. The driver walked up and grabbed them both by the arm. The assistant went to the back of the van to get a box of candy. Sally and Beth Ann did not resist and feigned fear.

"Oh, please don't hurt us!" Sally said.

"Yes, please don't hurt us, you big bad zombies," Beth Ann said.

They still did not resist when the driver moved them closer together, and the assistant tried to force a piece of candy into Sally's mouth.

The driver and the assistant both turned around when they were tapped on the shoulder. They looked down; Horace and Hector were smiling at them. The driver released the girls, and Hector jumped up and knocked him out with one mighty punch. The driver crumpled to the ground. Horace did the same to the assistant, and he collapsed on top of the driver. The box of candy spilled all over them.

The boys were excited and jumping around.

"Lights out!" Stanley said, punching the air. "That's the way I would have done it."

Rodney and Sammy did a high-five. Jackie did a celebration dance and shook his large stomach around. Magpo stuck his head out from Jackie's backpack and swung his arms.

"Bam-pow!" he said.

They rummaged through the back of the van and threw the candy onto the road. Sally found a box of Chocolate Dribble advertising balloons that the red-eyed workers would blow up and use to lure children.

"We might be able to use these balloons," Sally said to the others.

While the others were busy, Seth walked around to the front of the van and got in. He sat in the driver seat and closed the door. He looked out the window; no one was around. He picked up the van's two-way radio handset. He held it to his mouth and pushed the transmit button.

"Hello. Hello. Is anyone there?" he asked, speaking quietly.

He heard some static and then a voice.

"This is the warehouse dispatcher," the voice said in a monotone. "Do you have a question?"

Seth stopped and turned when he heard the door open. Horace was angry and staring up at him.

"Give me that," Horace said, holding his hand out.

Seth handed him the radio handset.

"No," Horace said, imitating the monotone of the dispatcher. "Mission continuing as planned."

"Copy," said the voice. "Stay off this line."

"Affirmative," Horace said, and he ended the transmission by pulling the handset's cord out.

"I thought there was something odd about you," Horace said.

Horace stepped up into the van, and Seth leaned away. Horace grabbed him by his collar and dragged him out of the van. Everyone gathered around.

"What's going on?" Sally asked.

"Hold him," Horace said to Hector.

Hector grabbed both of Seth's arms from behind and held him tight. Horace took Magpo from Jackie's backpack and held him in front of Seth's face. As Magpo started sniffing, Seth turned away.

"He smell funny," Magpo said. "He not human."

Horace put Magpo back in Jackie's backpack and walked back to Seth.

"Reveal your true form," he said.

"I don't know what you're talking about," Seth said.

"Very well," Horace said.

Horace grabbed Seth by the neck and squeezed. Seth began to strain for air, and Sally grabbed Horace's arm.

"What are you doing?" Sally asked.

"He is not what he seems," Horace said.

"What if you're wrong?" she asked.

"The Naked Katawamp's nose is never wrong," Horace said.

Seth's face turned bright red.

"Yeck, yeck," he said in a strange voice.

"Did you hear that?" Stanley asked nervously and sniffled.

"Whaoo, this is exorcism stuff!" Rodney said.

Sally and her friends were shocked when Seth's face started changing. Horace released his grip when Seth was revealed as the Goblin King's servant Seymour. Hector released him, and he fell to his knees.

"Yeck, yeck," he coughed and bent over.

"What is it?" Sally asked.

"Hector is a species expert," Horace said.

"It is a Ferraweasel," Hector explained. "It is an offshoot from the Weaselous giganticus family. It is quite a despicable creature. Thankfully, they are very rare."

"Tie him up," Horace said to Hector.

Hector ran to get some rope from the back of the van.

* * *

A REVELATION

Hector started the engine. He drove while Horace sat in the front passenger seat. Horace turned to the back of the van.

"Our time has come," he said. "We must act as one."

The entire gang sat in the back of the van with all of their gear. They all nodded their heads. They were nervous but anxious to get started.

"Let's go," Sally said.

CHAPTER 19

Showdown at the Candy Factory

Seymour was tied up and lying on the floor of the van. Jackie had one of his legs over him to keep him in place. When Hector hit the gas, the van jerked forward. He made a U-turn, and they drove to the candy factory. The driver and his assistant were unconscious, tied up, and lying comfortably next to Seymour.

They approached the candy factory. Hector slowed down and pulled the van to the side of the road. He drove behind the large road sign that advertised that the Somertown Candy Factory and home of the Chocolate Dribble was only a mile away. When the van was completely hidden, he stopped. Horace and Hector joined everyone at the back of the van. Sally and her friends got out of the van and stretched their muscles. Horace slammed the back door of the van and left Seymour and his cohorts inside.

They sat on the grass in a circle and discussed their plan of attack. There were questions and continuing discussions as each small detail was finalized and everyone was comfortable with their assigned roles. Repetition helped memorization, and they even stood up at times to playact their movements. Horace warned that even the best plan could break down and the team might have to think creatively and improvise. Everyone understood the importance of this advice. When they were done, Jackie opened the van door so everyone could get back in.

"Does anyone have anything to gag the prisoner?" Horace asked.

No one could think of anything.

"Wait a minute," Jackie said. "I've got something."

He took off his right shoe and pulled off his dirty sock.

"Eewwww!" Beth Ann said, and everyone else laughed.

Jackie stepped into the van and stuffed the smelly sock into Seymour's mouth. Seymour tried to resist but could do nothing to stop him. Stanley threw Jackie's shoe to him, and he sat to put it on. When he sat, he patted Seymour on his belly.

"That's not that bad, is it?" he asked with a smile.

"Huumph, huumph," Seymour replied as he tried to spit the sock out.

Sally and her friends climbed in to join Jackie and Seymour. Horace and Hector took their same positions in the front seat. Hector slowly drove back onto the road and headed for the candy factory.

Hector drove into the factory yard. A rolling metal garage door was open, so Hector simply drove into the warehouse. He drove all the way in and parked at the doorway to the manufacturing part of the factory. Two employees walked to the back of the van. They opened the rear doors and were surprised to see everyone standing with their staffs at the ready. Horace and Hector snuck behind the employees, pushed them into the van, and slammed the doors. Horace and Hector scanned the warehouse to make sure they were not being watched. The van rocked back and forth, and there were bangs, thumps, and groans. When the motion and noise stopped, they opened the doors. The two additional employees were unconscious and tied up. They were lying next to Seymour and the others. The cargo van was now crowded with bad guys.

Horace and Hector climbed into the van and closed the doors. Horace took some powder out of his pouch and rubbed it on all the walking staffs.

"This should help you fight with great might," he said with a smile as he carefully rubbed the powder on each staff.

Everyone left the van in single file and quietly went through the factory door. They all moved into position to begin the attack. Even Magpo joined them.

Seymour was pushing the gag out of his mouth with his tongue.

"Phaa, phaa," he said and spit it out. "Yeck, yeck."

He immediately began to gnaw on the ropes that bound his hands. His sharp teeth cut through the rope quickly. He untied himself and opened the van door.

"Yeck, yeck!" he yelled.

The warehouse employees looked at him for a moment, and then one of them pressed a red button on a control panel hanging on the wall. A loud buzzer went off, warning that something was wrong.

The Goblin King heard the buzzer and looked out of his office window. He saw the intruders moving around the perimeter of the factory and taking up positions. He picked up the handset for the factory's public address system and flipped a switch that turned off the buzzer.

"We have intruders," he calmly broadcasted to all on the factory floor. "Get them."

The red-eyed workers stopped what they were doing and looked around for their enemies. The gargoyles had been napping on the ledges of the metal rafters of the building. They dropped down in flight, carrying some Earbees. The Goblin King turned to Miss Mephisto, who had now taken her human-like form.

"You know what to do," he said.

A translucent creature rose from the wooden floor. It had been lying flat and perfectly blending into the floor's color and texture. It now stood and looked like a jellyfish in human form.

"Go," the Goblin King said to the creature and pointed to the office door.

The creature walked to the door, melted down, and flowed through the crack at the bottom.

The Goblin King walked to the desk and picked up a pot of black liquid. He held it out to Miss Mephisto and smiled. She dipped her long sharp claws into the liquid. She did this with both hands and then waved them in the air to dry.

Everyone started to take their positions on the factory floor. Hector tapped Horace on the shoulder and pointed to the office stairs. The creature had flowed down the stairs like clear thickened water and was now reforming at the bottom of the steps.

"Everyone look at the office steps," Horace said quietly to the group.

Sally and her friends looked over, transfixed by the forming creature.

"What is it?" Stanley said nervously and wiped his nose on his sleeve.

"It's a Cephalablob," Hector said. "It acts like a chameleon in three dimensions. It can sneak up on you and sting you. Always be on guard for its presence."

The creature walked into the shadow of the steps and blended into the background.

Horace held his right hand in the air. He lowered his thumb and then each finger one at a time. He then chopped his fist down, which was the signal for their plan to begin.

Rodney and Sammy ran to the control panel for the conveyor belt. Horace and Hector ran to the conveyor belt itself that was moving the candy. Jackie took position nearby at the large containers that held the nougat, fruit fillings, and cream. Sally, Beth Ann, and Stanley guarded the perimeter to protect the others. Magpo curled up to make himself small and hid in a dark corner along the factory wall. The Valakon shot into the air to attack the swarming gargoyles.

Rodney and Sammy twisted the dials on the control panel, and the conveyor belt stopped. It then started again but was going in reverse. Chocolate candies flowed back to the forming machine and the chocolate vats. The newly formed candies fell on top of the old as they piled up and fell to the floor.

"That's it," Rodney said. "Let's go."

They then ran to join Jackie at the filling vats. They pulled Chocolate Dribble advertising balloons from their pockets and began to fill them from taps on the side of the vats.

Sally, Beth Ann, and Stanley began to fight the first wave of employees who converged on their position. Sally was excited and satisfied with her effort when she knocked Arthur Meney on the head with her staff and sent him tumbling to the floor. She then quickly turned, knocked the gun from Officer MacNamara's hand, and quickly subdued him with a hard poke to the belly and then a hard knock to the head when he bent over to hold his stomach.

"Great work," Beth Ann yelled to Sally, and they smiled at each other for a moment before continuing the fight.

Stanley and Beth Ann were standing back to back and fighting hard with strong swings and precise thrusts of their staffs.

"Keep it up," Beth Ann said to Stanley.

"I'm trying," he breathlessly replied.

Sally and her friends fought like ninja warriors with their charmed staffs.

Rodney, Sammy, and Jackie began pelting employees with filled balloons. "Yeeahhh!" Rodney and Sammy screamed as they threw them.

"Bombs away!" Jackie yelled when he threw his first balloon. "Eat this Nuclear Nougat Blaster, you zombie freaks!"

The balloons exploded on their heads and blinded them with sticky nougat, jelly, and cream. The balloons that missed an employee smashed onto the floor and created a colorful slippery mess. Employees were sliding into each other, falling, and piling up on the floor. Magpo sniffed the air from his hiding spot. His nose and his greatest joy in life enabled him to conquer his fear. He inched forward and stuck his tongue out to taste the sweet fillings covering the factory floor.

Horace and Hector jumped onto the conveyer belt and rode it to the chocolate vats. They used their staffs to knock down any employee who approached them from either side of the belt.

The Valakon was keeping the gargoyles occupied. The Valakon was quicker and more nimble than the larger gargoyles. They were paralyzed by its speed. He bit them on the neck, but they did not turn to stone and crumble to the ground. The intelligent gargoyles had put metal collars around their necks to protect this vulnerable spot from the deadly bite of the Valakon. The Valakon improvised and administered painful bites to other parts of their bodies. Shrieks and wails filled the air above the factory floor, and victims retreated to the rafters to rest and nurse their wounds.

Sally and her friends fought brilliantly but started to be overwhelmed by the large number of attackers that kept coming.

"Look out!" Beth Ann yelled to Sally when she saw danger on her blind side.

A gargoyle snatched Sally's staff and flew into the air with it.

"No!" Sally said desperately, looking up.

Sally stood defenseless. The staff attacked the startled gargoyle. The staff hit the gargoyle on the head until the gargoyle released it. It dropped back into Sally's hands, and she immediately smashed a large employee that was about to grab her.

"Wow," Sally said, looking at her staff in amazement.

Rodney, Sammy, and Jackie ran out of their balloon ammunition. Their bombardment had been effective.

"Next phase of the plan," Sammy said to the others.

They grabbed their staffs and ran to join the others. They fought off the employees and the diving gargoyles. They formed a defensive line and moved along with the conveyer belt that carried Horace and Hector. They continued to battle until they all converged at the chocolate vats.

Horace jumped onto the chocolate vat. He grabbed onto a metal ladder that was welded onto its side. He climbed to the top and poured some of the powder from his pouch into the vat of chocolate. The black smoke stopped immediately. He jumped over to do the same for the second vat.

Everyone continued to fight. The gargoyles attacked, carrying Earbees. A gargoyle swooped in and dropped an Earbee at Hector's head. Hector swung his staff like a baseball bat and connected perfectly with the wide-eyed Earbee. He hit a home run, and the shrieking Earbee flew into the rafters.

"Perfect swing," Sally said to Hector.

Sally and her friends copied this excellent technique. Staffs were swinging, and Earbees were flying through the air. They hit pop-ups, line drives, home runs, and a few foul tips into the chocolate vats. One landed on the packaging conveyor belt, and the Earbee's flexible body was jammed into a small Chocolate Dribble box. It stared through the cellophane panel on the top as the bulging box continued down the line. If this had been a sport, they would have all made the All-Star Team. Before long, dazed and chocolate-covered Earbees were staggering around the factory floor, moaning. The Earbee assault was a complete failure.

Horace emptied his pouch into the second vat. An increasing number of zombie victims and gargoyles kept attacking. Sally and her friends retreated back closer and closer to the chocolate vats. People they knew from Somertown kept coming in from different areas of the plant.

Jackie's friend Corey Wilson stepped forward.

"I got this one," Jackie said. "Hey, Corey. How ya doin', buddy?"

Corey moved forward, and Jackie bopped him on the side of the head and knocked him out.

"Sorry about that, ol' buddy," Jackie said. "Nothing personal. You know how it is."

They fought valiantly but were being overrun. Sally began to believe that all was lost when she heard a loud cheer.

"It's the Baron!" Sally yelled with joy.

The Baron and Sister Mary, along with some of the older boys from Saint Bartholomew's Orphanage, came pouring in from the warehouse, carrying bats and hockey sticks. A large number of neighborhood dogs followed behind the Baron. They all formed a second front against the attackers. Sally and her friends fought with a renewed spirit when they saw that their friend was alive and had come back with reinforcements to help them.

Horace climbed down from the chocolate vat. He hung from the final rung of the ladder and then dropped to the floor. Hector turned to check on him and saw Miss Mephisto sneaking up on Horace with her claws out to attack.

"Look out!" Hector warned.

Hector ran and jumped in front of Horace's body. Miss Mephisto swung and sunk her claws deeply into Hector's back, and he screamed in pain. Horace turned, and Hector collapsed in his arms. Horace knelt down on one knee and gently laid Hector's body on the ground. Miss Mephisto smiled and raised her claws to swing again.

"Meeeowwww!" she screeched.

The Baron bit her in the back. He jerked her body violently back and forth with his powerful head and neck and threw her against a wall. She shrunk down into her cat form, turned pale white, and lay silent. She had a silly, dopey look on her face.

Horace bent down. "Thank you, Hector," he said.

"It was my honor, sir," Hector said weakly and closed his eyes.

Horace reached for his pouch. He opened it over Hector and shook it. Only a small amount of powder came out. It landed on Hector, glowed a bright gold color, and faded away. Horace leaned in and blew some air into Hector's lungs to resuscitate him. Hector did not move.

"Is he dead?" the Baron asked sadly.

Horace had tears in his eyes. He put his hand on Hector's wrist and his ear to his mouth.

"Not yet," he said. "There is still a chance."

Horace looked up and scanned the area. He picked up Hector and ran to the freezer that stored the ingredients for the chocolate. The Baron guarded him the whole way.

The battle continued, but they were all tiring from the onslaught. Even the Baron was becoming fatigued.

"I can't go much longer," Stanley said breathing heavily.

"We have to keep fighting," Sally said. "We can't give up."

The gargoyles and workers had driven Sister Mary and the Saint Bartholomew kids to one end of the factory. Sally and her friends were being attacked from land and air. They were isolated at the opposite end. They kept fighting, but they were losing ground.

The surge from the attackers backed them toward the wall of the factory. The Cephalablob appeared from the wall and grabbed Beth Ann.

"Noooo!" Stanley screamed.

An electric shock buzzed, and the Cephalablob and Beth Ann lit up, and her long hair stood straight up from the shock. Sally stood nearby, and her hair stood on end also. The creature released her, and she fell to the ground. She lay silent with her eyes closed. Stanley ran to help her; he became the Cephalablob's second victim. He fell down next to Beth Ann. The Cephalablob looked up and saw the Valakon flying at it. It quickly ran into the wall and disappeared.

The Valakon landed and walked along the wall and touched it at times but could not find the Cephalablob. Magpo joined the search and sniffed along the wall. He reached a chair that was sitting against the wall and stopped. Magpo sniffed the leg of the chair. He then turned to the Valakon, twitched his head toward the leg, and winked. The Valakon quickly flew in and bit down on the chair leg.

"Eeeeahhh!" the Cephalablob screamed in a high-pitched tone. It buzzed, and its body lit up along with the Valakon's. It stood up from where it had camouflaged itself as a chair and ran screaming out of the factory with some dogs in pursuit. The Valakon was unharmed.

Sally had gone to aid Beth Ann and Stanley. She was kneeling down next to them when the Goblin King grabbed her by the arm. He grabbed her staff and smashed it against a pipe. It splintered and broke in half. He raised her up and pulled her back close to his body. He held his sharp fingernails up to her neck.

"It's time to end this little party," he yelled. "Drop your weapons."

Both sides stopped and gathered around Sally and the Goblin King. The Baron stepped forward and growled.

"Don't do anything stupid, you smelly beast, or this girl will be dead," he said.

The Baron backed away, and Horace returned from the freezer.

"Let her go. It's me you want," he said.

"I'm greedy," he said with a smile and a snicker. "I want you both now. You in the Pit of Woe and she as my servant. I rather like her extraordinary spirit. I will have much joy in breaking it."

The Goblin King looked up and smiled.

"Let them come forward," he said, holding his hand up and waving it toward himself.

The crowd of red-eyed people and gargoyles parted, and Sally's parents walked forward. Her father was carrying a box of chocolates.

"Mom, Dad, no," she said, shaking her head and crying.

"Mom, Dad, yes," the Goblin King said with great glee.

Her father cupped his left hand behind her neck and held the box of chocolates with his right. Her mother slowly took a piece of candy from the box and placed it against Sally's lips. Sally cried and looked into her mother's eyes. The red cleared from her eyes, and she blinked.

"Sally," she said.

"It's me, Mom," Sally said.

Her father's eyes cleared, and he let her head go.

"What is this?" the Goblin King yelled angrily and looked around. All of his victims' eyes were beginning to clear.

"How?" the Baron asked Horace.

"It was the black smoke that kept them under the spell," Horace replied. "The smoke has finally cleared."

The Goblin King turned to the confused gargoyles.

"Get them!" he ordered.

The ground began to rumble, and the walls of the factory shook. The gargoyles started to vibrate.

"Stand down, my errant children," the Rock Lord said in a loud, deep voice that came from the rock walls of the factory.

The factory and the gargoyles were both made from Somertown rocks. The gargoyles heard and felt the Rock Lord's words, and they knew what he could do. They stood down.

The Goblin King held onto Sally even tighter when his control of the others was gone. He was isolated with no one left to support him. Even Miss Mephisto was injured and unable to help. Seymour just stood and watched along with the gargoyles. There was nothing he could do.

"Stay back," the Goblin King said, pressing his sharp nails to Sally's neck and looking around for any sign of aggression. Seeing none, he smiled and began to back up.

"Owwww," he screamed. He turned around and dropped his nails from Sally's neck.

Magpo took a bite of the Goblin King's right ankle. The Goblin King kicked his leg out, but Magpo held on. This action produced another more intense shot of pain for the Goblin King every time he kicked. His weak ankles were his Achilles' heel.

"Owwww, you little—owwww!" the Goblin King screamed.

Sally kicked back with her left leg and smashed the heel of her boot into the Goblin King's left ankle. Horace moved quickly and snatched Sally away from the hobbled Goblin King.

Magpo released the Goblin King's leg and scampered to safety. The Goblin King ran away quickly and dodged a lunge made by the Baron. Even in great pain and limping slightly, the Goblin King was swift and agile. He picked up Miss Mephisto and ran into the warehouse. In the paved yard in front of the warehouse the air started to bubble and foam. A large circle about ten feet in diameter formed. It was the same blue-green color and consistency as the circle at the mall. The bottom of the foaming, bubbling circle touched the blacktop of the yard. An escape exit to the Goblin King's world was now ready to be used. The Goblin King ran out of the warehouse and cackled because he knew he and Miss Mephisto would soon be safe in another time and space.

Horace used his exceptional speed to pursue the Goblin King. He was making up ground, but the Goblin King was getting very close to the portal. The Goblin King turned around a few times to check on Horace's progress. He was worried but calmed down when he was about twenty feet to freedom. The Goblin King laughed and leaped into the bubbling, foaming circle.

Horace caught up to him at this moment and reached into the foam as the Goblin King's trailing left leg disappeared. Horace stood in this position for a moment and strained to back up. With great effort Horace was able to take two steps backward. His arm and hand appeared out of the foam. He had a tight hold on the Goblin King's ankle and was pulling him back. The Goblin King tried to kick free, but Horace held on.

The Baron was next to arrive, and he also grabbed the Goblin King's leg. They both pulled hard, and the Goblin King and Miss Mephisto popped back into Somertown. The Baron lifted the Goblin King to his feet, turned him around, wrapped both of his arms around his chest, and held him tight. Miss Mephisto fell from the Goblin King's arms, and Horace caught her.

The Goblin King tried to wriggle free. The Baron lifted him off the ground and growled. The Goblin King stopped struggling and froze when he felt the Baron's hot breath and the sharp touch of teeth on the back of his neck. The Goblin King's body slumped in the Baron's arms, and he gave up. Horace placed Miss Mephisto in the Goblin King's hands, and he seemed grateful.

All the others, including a revived Beth Ann and Stanley, caught up and watched. Sally and her friends, her parents, the candy factory employees, and the people of Somertown were all relieved. The gargoyles were the only ones who were nervous.

"Everything that belongs in the Goblin King's world will go back to that world," Horace said. He turned to the gargoyles. "You will go too and remain alive in that world."

The gargoyles looked at each other. They smiled, and nodded their heads. They were pleased and grateful.

"You will come with me, my friend," Horace said to the Baron. "I will need your help for a while."

"Yes, of course," the Baron said.

"I will get Hector, and we will go," Horace said.

The Baron held onto the Goblin King, and Horace went to get Hector. The Valakon flew up and landed on the Baron's right shoulder. Magpo crawled up his leg and back and sat on his left shoulder.

"I'm going to miss you and your friends," the Baron said to Sally. "But I will return. I will be in my true form, so I tell you now that I love you, Sally. When I come back, I will not be able to talk, but I will show that love through actions."

Sally began to cry again. "We love you too," she said and hugged Beth Ann who was also crying.

"Us too," Stanley said, standing with Rodney, Sammy, and Jackie.

"And me," Sister Mary said.

The Baron smiled.

Horace walked back, carrying Hector. Ice crystals had formed on Hector's hair and eyebrows. Horace laid him gently on the ground. He then hugged Sally.

"I love you, Sally," he said. "You are brave and strong."

"I love you too," Sally said.

Horace waved goodbye to Sally's friends and picked up Hector. He moved closer to the bubbling circle in the air.

"Gargoyles and those from the Goblin King's world step forward. Everyone else back away," he said.

Everyone complied. The Valakon flew from the Baron's shoulder into Sally's arms. It snuggled in and got comfortable. Sally smiled when it looked up at her with its big brown eyes.

Horace with Hector and the Baron with the Goblin King, Miss Mephisto, and Magpo walked closer to the portal. Horace turned to Sally.

"Don't be sad. Try to be glad," he said with a smile. "If you're in danger, I won't be a stranger."

Sally smiled, and Magpo waved goodbye. Sally's friends waved and said goodbye. Horace and the Baron stepped into the bubbles and disappeared.

A vortex appeared in front of the hole in space like a small inverted tornado, and it began to spin faster and faster and grow larger and larger. The gargoyles, Earbees, Cephalablob, Seymour, and every Hibernating Hopping Heart Beetle were sucked into the hole in the center of the vortex. It grew larger, turned toward the ground, and rose up into the sky. Like a giant vacuum cleaner it began to suck the black smoke in.

Sally and her friends watched as everything related to the Goblin King's world was sucked in. The Feral Devils and the Spiny Vacusuckers rose into the sky and twirled in circles as they were pulled into the vortex. The Vacusuckers tried to use their suction to stay, but they could not resist the powerful vortex. Every last Cedebeast, Bingbat Bug, Aquacane, Giant Worm, Spikyblinder, and Terraglider rose up to the sky. Even the injured Narcisserpent appeared in the sky and was sucked in.

The vortex seemed to know that a balance had been upset and that these things did not belong. In less than a minute the vortex sucked back into the fizzing, foaming bubbles. This large circle shrunk to a point in the air and then disappeared

SHOWDOWN AT THE CANDY FACTORY

entirely. Everyone and everything that had managed to cross worlds by choice or chance was now gone. The Valakon shrunk down and turned back into a small toy that Sally latched onto her belt loop.

CHAPTER 20

Back to Normal

Sally sat on the desk chair in her bedroom. She bent over and tied the laces on her black hiking boots. She walked to her bureau, grabbed the Valakon, and clipped it to the belt loop of her blue jeans. She ran out of her room and down the stairs. She grabbed her green coat from the closet at the bottom of the stairs and walked into the living room. Her father was reading the newspaper on the sofa.

"Hey, Dad, what's up?" she asked.

"Whitley Snit was arrested again," John replied and laughed.

Sally laughed with him as her mother walked into the living room.

"Where are you going?" she asked.

"I'm going to hang out with my friends at the rocks," she replied.

"Be home for dinner," Amanda said, sitting down on the sofa and picking up her Pineman and the Young Geniuses book from the coffee table.

"I will," Sally said.

Sally ran out the door and up the long hill in front of her house. It was a bright, clear day, and the sun was shining beautifully. Her friends were waiting for her at the Saint Bartholomew rocks at the top of the hill. They were all there.

Beth Ann, Stanley, Rodney, Sammy, and Jackie Chambers all waved to her as she came closer.

"Hey, guys," she said and sat down on the rocks.

They all looked at her.

"What?" she asked.

"We were all talking about something before you came," Rodney said. "How come you never told us all about Horace?"

"I didn't think you would believe me," she said.

"You're right," Sammy said. "He was bigger than life and out of control."

"I don't know," Stanley said. "I might have believed you. We did see him do some amazing things last Christmas. We knew he was special."

"And there were those rumors after you were in the hospital," Beth Ann said. "I heard all sorts of stories when I came back from my Christmas trip to Japan."

"You're right," Stanley said. "We should have been able to figure it out or at least ask better questions."

"But you did mislead us when you said he went back home," Beth Ann said.

"He did go back home," Sally said with a sly smile. "And, besides, you know everything now."

"What about that little Hector?" Jackie asked. "He was tough. Do you think he made out okay?"

Everyone was quiet for a moment.

"I don't know," Sally said. "I hope so."

"And the Baron?" Rodney asked.

"Do you think he'll ever come home?" Stanley asked.

"I don't know that either," Sally replied, shaking her head.

"I liked that little Naked Katawamp Magpo," Beth Ann said. "At first I thought he was ugly and cowardly, but when I got to know him I realized he was really cute and brave. You know—like Stanley."

Stanley was embarrassed, and everyone laughed.

"I really liked fighting with those sticks," Jackie said, launching into a mock battle with Rodney and Sammy. They traded a few blows before stopping.

"I was thinking about joining a martial arts class," Jackie said, grabbing his stomach with his right hand. "I could get in better shape and really learn how to fight."

"That's a pretty good idea." Stanley said. "We should all do it together."

"That is a good idea," Beth Ann said, walking close to Stanley and smiling. "We can be in the same class."

"Uh, yeah," Stanley said, getting a little nervous when Beth Ann entered his personal space. "That's what I just said."

"Remember when you saved me?" she asked.

"Of course," Stanley said, blushing.

"Owwww—aaahhh!" Sammy said. "Stanley saved the love of his life."

He turned to Rodney and puckered his lips. They smacked kisses at each other from a distance, and Sammy spoke in a high voice. "Oh, Stanley, my hero. You saved me."

"Shut up," Stanley said as everyone laughed.

"Hey," Sally said, changing the subject to save Stanley from any further embarrassment. "Is everybody wearing the same costume for the Halloween dance?"

"Yes," Beth Ann said. "I already got that information. Except Jackie doesn't think he's coming to the dance."

"I really don't like dances," Jackie said. "It's not my thing."

"Come on, Jackie. You have to come. You're part of the team," Sally said.

"Yeah, man, you have to be there," Rodney said. "You have to reevaluate that position."

"No question," Sammy said.

Beth Ann and Stanley nodded their heads.

"I don't know," Jackie said. "Is there going to be any food?"

"Raw veggies with dip," Beth Ann said.

"Aaaahhh!" Jackie screamed. "I'm not going."

Everyone laughed. Sally spoke up and made a more appealing pitch to Jackie.

"We'll also have pizza and tacos," Sally said. "And free Chocolate Dribbles."

"Did you hear that, buddy?" Jackie said, patting his belly. "Now they're talking our language. That bad Beth Ann was not giving you the whole story."

Craaackkk!

A bolt of lighting streaked through the sky, and the ground rumbled. Everyone was quiet for a moment.

"What the heck was that?" Stanley asked and sniffled.

"I don't know," Sally said. "But I think something might be happening."

"The Goblin King?" Beth Ann asked.

"No," Sally said, smiling. "Something good."

"Look!" Jackie said, pointing down the hill.

In the distance a figure was running up the hill. Rodney stood up from the rocks. He had the best eyesight in the group. He looked intently for a long moment and then smiled.

"It's the Baron!" he yelled.

They all jumped down from the rocks. They whooped in glee and pumped their arms in the air. Sally and Beth Ann hugged each other and smiled.

Baron Von Muncher reached them and jumped up on Sally. He knocked her to the ground and licked her face. Sally held her hands up and laughed. Everyone gathered around. Stanley hugged Beth Ann, and Sammy slapped Rodney's hand. Stanley then turned and held up his hand to slap Jackie's.

Jackie didn't slap his hand. He held his arms out and raised his eyebrows. Stanley tried to back up, but Jackie grabbed him in a strong hug and lifted him off the ground.

Stanley was being crushed by Jackie's enthusiastic hug. Stanley slapped Jackie on the shoulder.

"Can't...can't breathe," he said, struggling to talk.

"Oh, sorry," Jackie said. He gently put him down, and Stanley gulped for air.

They all played with the Baron. They tumbled and rolled on the ground. They finished playing and then all sat on the hill. The Baron was tired after everything he had been through. He lay on his side while Jackie petted him.

"Remember when we thought he was dead?" Jackie asked.

"That was the saddest day," Beth Ann said.

"I knew he would beat that serpent," Stanley said.

"Liar. You said he was dead, and you cried," Sammy said.

"I meant that he was probably a little dead," Stanley said.

"Aaaahh!" Beth Ann screamed. "You drive me crazy. You can't be a little dead."

"You know I just like to keep my options open," Stanley said, frowning.

"That's why we love you," Beth Ann said, patting him on the cheek, and Stanley smiled.

"She said she looooves him," Jackie said, swooning. Everyone laughed, and Baron Von Muncher barked.

Sally sat quietly and stared down the hill. Beth Ann moved over to Sally and hugged her. "Great day," she said.

Sally nodded. "Everything is almost perfect," she said.

"You're thinking about Horace and Hector aren't you?" Beth Ann asked.

"You always worry about things you don't know," Sally replied.

"Let's hope for the best," Beth Ann said, grabbing her hand.

"I will," Sally said, squeezing her hand.

It was getting late. Everyone said their goodbyes and started to walk down the hill in different directions. Sally walked down with Beth Ann and Baron Von Muncher.

"Hey," Beth Ann said.

"What?" Sally asked.

"What do you think happened to that old Goblin King?"

"I don't know."

CHAPTER 21

The Goblin King's New Normal

The gargoyles perched around the top branches of the Goblin King's tree. The darkness was starting to clear, and the sun was shining through the clouds. The Goblin King's room was empty. Down below the ground where the roots had kept the Telesee-ers captive a new reality existed. The Goblin King, Miss Mephisto (now back to black), and Seymour were now entangled and trapped by the roots.

A pair of gargoyles rolled the flat polished stone from the Goblin King's room into the underground chamber. They set it on its side in front of the Goblin King and his unfortunate aids. The Telesee-ers reached out to take hold of the stone. They were no longer covered in dirt. Though strange looking, they were regal and elegant. They stood seven feet tall with large, bulbous, hairless white heads but human-sized handsome faces. They wore brilliant white robes that flowed to the ground. Their long, thin fingers took hold of the side of the rock, and an image appeared. Horace and Santa Claus sat smiling. The Naked Katawamp Magpo sat on Santa's lap and waved. Everything was right in their world. The Goblin King's body slumped, and he sank down.

"Please, no," he begged.

"Yeck, yeck," Seymour said.

The Telesee-ers smiled and continued to project the image on the rock.

CHAPTER 22

The Trick-or-Treat Ball

The planning for the Halloween dance was a major success. The dance was in the school gymnasium, which was wonderfully decorated. They agreed to name the dance the "Trick-or-Treat Ball" and put it on a banner that hung over the entrance. Sally and her planning team kept things traditional with witch, black cat, goblin, skeleton, vampire, werewolf, and zombie characters decorating the walls. Kids from the art department made gargoyle figures from paper and glue and hung them from the ceiling along with the Goblin King in a cage. His hands were clutching the bars, and his face looked miserable. They all lazily swung as air circulated through the room. They also made a 3-D mummy character that looked like it was breaking through the wall at the entrance to the dance. Everyone posed for pictures next to the mummy that was trying to grab them.

Winged jack-o'-lantern centerpieces adorned the tables. The food, served buffet-style, included raw veggies with dip, fruit, pizza, tacos, mini-sandwiches, and pumpkin pie. There was also plenty of Chocolate Dribbles and candy corn. Every flavor of soda was provided along with a "Witches Brew" punch made from a mixture of fruit juices with jelly worms floating about. A band and a disc jockey provided the music.

The event was sold out, and everyone came in costume. Officer MacNamara was there for security but was dressed as a penitentiary prisoner. Sister Mary was a nurse. Her beautiful brown hair, usually hidden by her habit and veil, was proudly on display and pinned up under her nurse cap. Her hair was a great curiosity to everyone at the dance. Mr. Strickland was Paul Bunyan with a plastic axe. Sally's parents were Superman and Wonder Woman. The Dribbles were dressed as the three blind mice with mouse ears, painted-on whiskers, tails, and dark glasses. Arthur Meney was dressed as Daddy Warbucks. He had pulled a rubber baldhead disguise over the last remaining hair on the sides of his head. Baron Von Muncher sat at the entrance to the gymnasium. He was wearing one of Officer MacNamara's old police shirts that Sally and Beth Ann had cut and sewed to fit his body. He made sure to keep a watch on everyone.

Sally and her friends wore their same costumes. They had freshened them up since their adventure. Rodney and Sammy were now reconnected in their Day of the Dead Siamese Twin costume. Jackie Chambers wore his green robe cinched around his waist by a rope. He now carried the staff that he used for his battles. A cute girl dressed as a princess stared at him for a moment.

"What are you, a giant elf?" she asked.

"No," Jackie replied.

"Irish Jedi."

"No."

"I give up."

"Friar Tuck," Jackie said with a smile and began to talk to the princess.

Sally was having a good time but was reserved and not her usual self.

"You're thinking about them, aren't you?" Beth Ann asked.

"Yes. I can't stop. I'm still worried," Sally replied.

"I'm sure they're fine," Beth Ann said. "Let's go get some food. They have plenty of veggies."

"And pizza," Sally said with a smile.

"Of course, pizza," Beth Ann said.

They walked to the buffet table.

Sally and her friends sat at their round table with their plates of food. Jackie had two enormous plates of pizza and tacos. The band started a slow song.

"Let's dance," Beth Ann said to Stanley.

"I don't know. I have all this food," Stanley said.

Jackie poked Stanley with his elbow and almost knocked him off his chair.

"Don't be such a Halloweeney. Dance with the pretty girl," he said.

"Okay," Stanley said, rubbing his arm.

Beth Ann smiled, and Stanley grabbed her hand. They walked to the dance floor, and Jackie slid Stanley's plate of food over to his own. They did a slow dance next to Sally's parents and Arthur Meney, who was dancing with Minnie Dribble.

The slow dance ended, and the band started playing "The Monster Mash." Rodney and Sammy grabbed Sally's arm.

"Let's dance," they said.

"Come on, Jackie," Sally said, jumping up.

"In a minute," Jackie said, staring at his food. "I have some important business here."

The dance floor filled. Everyone was dancing wildly and having a great time.

"You are one witchy woman," Sammy said to Sally.

"Shut up, Sammy," she said, laughing, and continued to dance.

Jackie joined them on the dance floor before the song ended. He teamed up with the princess. Jackie was an excellent dancer, but when he moved his big belly around, he kept bumping into Stanley. Stanley was having such a great time that he refused to let anything bother him. He would just get back in stride and continue dancing. Everyone shared Stanley's attitude, and they all had a wonderful time at the dance.

CHAPTER 23

A COMFORTING END

It had been a long night, and Sally walked up the steps to go to bed. Her parents relaxed on the sofa.

"Good night," Amanda said.

"Great dance," John said.

"Thanks," Sally said. "Good night."

She walked to her bureau. She unclipped the Valakon from her belt loop and placed it next to her secret box.

She started to pull her witch costume over her head but stopped when she heard a noise. Her secret box had fallen to the floor, and her diary had tumbled out. It was open to the page where Horace's blank fortune was kept. She picked up the diary, and there was writing on the page.

"Hector is fine long live rhyme. When you are older we will toast with wine. Love, Horace"

Sally looked up and smiled at the Valakon.

THE END

Glossary of Otherworldly Strangeness
(BY ORDER OF APPEARANCE)

Bingbat Bug (bing-bat bug) a bright blue spidery bug with three black dots on its back. If a line were traced connecting all three dots, it would form a perfect triangle. It is the size of a child's fist and produces a silky material that is both super-strong and fireproof. The bite of this bug will paralyze the victim, which it then wraps in its silky excretion to be consumed later. It does not form a web to ensnare victims but attacks by jumping from bushes, leaping from behind or under rocks, and dropping from trees. Their prey can be as large as a child. Experts can harvest the excretion to weave thread to make virtually indestructible clothing.

Cedabeast (se-da-beast) a mammal about the size of a very large and extraordinarily muscular bull. The head is similar to that of a male lion but much larger, with a black mane. It does not have whiskers or fur. The skin on its face and body is black, leathery, and difficult to penetrate. The Cedabeast is surprisingly fast for its size. It is an omnivore and will eat anything. It dispatches its prey by biting and ripping with its mouthful of shark-like teeth. If bitten, the prey will die shortly even if it escapes because the Cedabeast's teeth are coated with poisonous saliva. The black hoofs and bones of the animal are very dense and hard. They can be used to manufacture eating and cooking utensils as well as polished knife handles and protective plating.

Hibernating Hopping Heart Beetle (hi-ber-nat-ing hop-ping heart bee-tle) a black beetle between one and two inches in diameter when fully grown. The beetles hibernate under the ground for ten years. They awaken for six months to eat and breed before returning to hibernation. Their sharp teeth and pincers are used to kill prey. Female beetles carry their eggs during hibernation. Upon waking, they chew into a living victim and lay eggs on the heart. The beetle and the hatchlings then devour the heart and the host. The female beetles can be used as a weapon to dispatch an opponent. The female is carefully dug from the ground and kept in a comfortable pouch. The beetle can be thrown at an opponent. The impact on a warm body causes the beetle to awaken and begin chewing. This technique causes your opponent to die in an extraordinarily agonizing way.

Spikyblinder (spi-key blind-er) small spiky-headed creatures with no eyes. They are blind and mute but have a keen sense of hearing and smell. Diet consists mainly of grubs.

Terraglider (ter-ra-glid-er) bird-like creatures that can't fly well but are excellent divers and gliders. Spikyblinders are their main prey.

Telesee-ers (tel-e-see-ers) seven-foot-tall beings with large, bulbous, hairless white heads with small human-sized faces.

They have long thin fingers that can project images on smooth objects through the power of thought.

Ferraweasel (fer-ra-weas-el) a rare obnoxious creature with the head of a ferret and the body of a small child. It is an offshoot from the Weaselous giganticus family. Their diet consists of anything edible that can be stolen.

Valakon (val-a-kon) an elfin animal with the head of a Yorkshire Terrier and the body of a flying squirrel with a bobbed tail. It has large eyes that can change colors and raccoon-like hands. This animal is very rare and can bring you luck when you need it most.

Gargoyle (gar-goyle) a grotesquely carved figure. In the case at hand they were carved of stone and adorned the buildings in the Saint Bartholomew's Orphanage complex. They came to life through an external evil action. This was a pleasant surprise to the normally quite sedentary stone objects, and they enjoyed their ability to move, fly, and interact with the world. This was opposed to their previous passive interaction with rain, sleet, snow, wind, and bird droppings. In living form they are clannish but have individual looks, colors, and personalities.

Earbees (ear-bees) about two feet tall, these creatures have the look of a giant serving of chocolate custard. They have a somewhat gelatinous composition in that they are very flexible and moldable but do not break apart. They have black beady eyes, small mouths, and sharp teeth. They have stick-thin tiny legs and arms but large hands with exceptionally long thin index fingers. Their limbs are a lighter shade of brown than their bodies, except the palms of their hands are blood red. If they get their index fingers into a victim's ears, they can take control of the brain and thus the body.

Rock Lord (rock lord) the sentient energy and intelligence that exists in all rocks on Earth but is unknown by humans.

Giant Worms (gi-ant worms) giant worms that live in and absorb nutrients from soil.

Naked Katawamp (na-ked ka-ta-wamp) a small creature that looks like a large hairless rat with pinkish white skin and dark pink eyes. It squeals when scared but is very intelligent and capable of human speech. The Katawamp lives in close family units of ten to twenty animals. It can live above or below ground and has an extremely acute sense of smell. It is always looking for a good meal. Typically, it forages at night to avoid predators. The Naked Katawamp smells like freshly popped popcorn.

Feral Devil (fe-ral dev-il) a vicious pack animal with the head of a wolf and a body like a muscular miniature pony. It has sharp teeth and fangs that can easily rip open any living thing. The pack hunts together and uses encircling methods to trap and attack prey. A pack can have as many as fifteen members or more.

Spiny Vacusucker (spi-ney vac-u-suck-er) a large pack animal that emits a strong odor; quite frankly, they stink. The animals have dots on the front of their bodies like a leopard and stripes in the back like a zebra. The dots are black on white skin, and the stripes are black on orange skin. Their skin has the consistency and texture of an elephant's, and they also have a trunk like an elephant's. They have a large, wide mouth below the trunk, spiny backs, and are about the size of a hippopotamus. Their loud, high-pitched screams can shatter eardrums. They capture their prey by creating a powerful suction with their trunks. Air is sucked in and expelled through a blowhole on their backs. Once trapped by the suction at the end of their trunks, the unfortunate prey is popped into the mouth and travels alive to the stomach for a slow digestion process.

Aquacane (aq-ua cane) animal that resembles a smaller-than-usual Chihuahua with a coat of short black hair and bright incandescent green eyes. It also has a set of gills like a fish, clearly visible under each ear. The animal initially lived only on land but evolved to be equally comfortable in the water. Aquacanes travel in packs and constantly search for food on land and in water. Their surprisingly large appetites far outweigh their size, and they will eat anything they can fit in their mouths. They are known for making a distinctive high-pitched chirping sound—"Cha-heek. Cheek-cheek-cheek."

Narcisserpent (nar-cis-ser-pent) a giant, poisonous black serpent with identical heads at each end of its body. This animal can grow to over forty feet in length. It has large fangs and long flicking tongues. Each identical head is hopelessly in love with the other. Their favorite activity is to intertwine their bodies until the two heads are staring at each other. The two heads will flick their tongues out until they touch. The two heads of the Narcisserpent can spend hours staring into each other's eyes and admiring the rare beauty.

Cephalablob (ceph-a-la-blob) the creature is a translucent blob of material with the texture of a jellyfish. The blob can stretch and take different form, color, and texture. It acts like a chameleon in three dimensions. The creature can emit a strong electro-magnetic shock that is powerful enough to stop the heart and kill.

Enjoy These Previews from Chapters of

HELPING HORACE HELFIN

BOOK THREE IN THE HORACE HELFIN SERIES

CHAPTER 1

THE SHADOWY STRANGER

The dark figure sat in the shadows. It spoke slowly and deliberately.

"Tell them what they want to hear. Promise them… everything. Once you obtain power, you can do what you want."

The small men with small minds listened intently and nodded their heads as if in a trance.

CHAPTER 2

A Stranger Comes to Town

The skinny, haggard white-haired man walked slowly down the street on a warm July day. He was clean-shaven but had vacant eyes, and his green suit was wrinkled and worn. He seemed to be lost or homeless. He stopped at a fine house on a fine street. He stared at the door and the street number for a moment and then walked to the front door. He breathed in deeply, exhaled slowly, and knocked three times.

Sally Connors opened the door and stared up at the sullen man. Deep in Sally's mind there was a tiny glimmer of recognition, but she could not make the connection.

"Can I help you?" she asked.

"Hello, Sally," he replied. "I'm Santa Claus, and I need your help."

ABOUT THE AUTHOR

John Philip McCarthy is an attorney born in Philadelphia, Pennsylvania.

ABOUT THE ARTIST

Paulette Bensignor is a classically trained artist with a studio in Pennsylvania. She was born in Philadelphia, Pennsylvania. Her work can be seen at her website and in a number of public and private collections in the United States, Europe, and Asia.

www.bensignor.com

BOATHOUSE ENTERTAINMENT
PRESENTS
THE AWARD-WINNING

Horace Helfin
SERIES OF BOOKS

2011 International Book Awards Winner
2010 Readers Favorite Awards Winner
2010 USA "Best Books" Finalist
2010 National Indie Excellence Finalist

Available in paperback and e-book at your local bookstore, bn.com or amazon.com

www.HoraceHelfin.com
Boathse@gmail.com

The third book in the series will be available soon:
Helping Horace Helfin